HOTEL AAN ZEE AND THE TURBULENT FORCES OF LOVE

Joachim Frank

Printed in the United States of America
Hardcover ISBN: 979-8-9997389-0-5
Paperback ISBN: 979-8-9997389-1-2
Ebook ISBN: 979-8-9997389-2-9

CHAPTER 1

"No wise man can tie water into a knot on the edges of his garment/ No sage knows the number of grains of sand on earth"
—*from Ifa Divination Poetry*

As he was operating the xerox machine, Hubert stared out of the window of the library onto a pompous landscape made of marble. The architecture—monolithic, posturing, enduring—was Hitler's unacknowledged redemption in the very country that had fought him to death. Young students with bleached sneakers crossed the plaza. In the absence of a breeze, the flag on the big pole was tired; the stars and stripes were jumbled up and half-hidden in the folds of the fabric.

Hubert copied a page of the International Science Citation Index. It listed the citations of his own work by other scientists: an entire page-long column in the finest print. He received great satisfaction from seeing his work acknowledged; the heaviness of these orange-colored volumes seemed to signify the profound mark he had left in the history of human endeavor. Studying the page he had just copied, he was quite startled to realize that the Belovski, H. listed there was, in reality, the composite of four scientists, only one of whom was himself. The decision of the publishers to list initials rather than first names for economy had thrown together the scientific output of four Belovskis who were probably at odds with one another in all imaginable attributes, such as hairstyle, age, and habitat. What was worse, every trace of gender was lost, and the initial H. had become a fountain of two streams of speculations sharply divided by the sex of their bearers: namely one including all those dull co-Huberts, Herberts, Henrys, and Hanks and the other one sparkling with Henriettas, Heathers, Hildegards, and Helgas.

The first H. Belovski, in neurophysiology, had jumped onto the stage sometime in 1963. There was a seemingly timid H. Belovski in the field of agriculture who had launched a paper in 1967 on the use of pesticides in the Finger Lakes, which was widely cited for a brief period but then disappeared into oblivion. Meanwhile, the neuro-physiological Belovski had gathered quite a following, as witnessed by twenty-odd papers in reputable journals, until, presumably, a high administrative position separated him from his coauthors' quest for truth. He might have become a functionary in some professional society, administrator of grant monies, co-editor of journals with names that had a pregnant sound to them, such as *Nerve, Soul, Self,* or *Applied Conscience.*

During the decline of the second Belovski's scientific output, H. Belovski proper stepped in, the one whose H. stood for "Hubert." At once, he recognized his papers in the physics of turbulence; he was still proud of his first article which was entitled "The Birth of a Twister." He was one of those scientists of whom it is said that they are spending their life proving their Ph.D. thesis right, and the birth of the twister gave rise to many afterbirths in papers, letters to the editor, abstracts, and reviews, finally to be crowned by a monograph on "A Twister's Sudden Birth," subtitled "The Onset of Turbulent Phenomena in Meteorology." The book was a phenomenal flop; it earned him exactly $324.50 in royalties before it disappeared from the bookshelves for good.

The fourth H. Belovski was a curious fellow who dwelled on organic compounds. He worked himself up from two-ring compounds to those with three and five and then landed himself safely in the lap of a pharmaceutical company.

What Hubert had never hoped to accomplish in his lifetime materialized in front of his eyes: here was the true genius H. Belovski, beloved scholar of arts and letters, equally accomplished in fields as widely separated as the science of the grain and the science of the brain. The Science Citation Index had created a universal mind bearing his very own name. Coming centuries, unable to grasp the subtleties of citation listings in the twentieth century and the obliterating need for economy, would rank him with none less than Leonardo da Vinci.

He had the sensation of standing in an enormous cathedral and feeling dwarfed by the columns and beams of light coming in from the windows, though in reality, he was a nothing, a speck of dust that was barely visible and could be blown away by the whisper of a prayer.

"Operator, operator, out of paper," the xerox machine screamed.

A red light started flashing, demanding attendance by an unspecified operator, much like a little boy who gets in trouble and calls his mother by her generic name. Hubert pressed a button to activate a tiny bell that was used on this occasion. Anticipating the approach of benevolently smiling library personnel, he hastily hid the traces of his self-indulgence under one of the heavy volumes. When the motherly figure of the senior duplication technician arrived, Hubert found himself unequipped to answer the question he was sure to be asked: what kind of business had caused the machine to run out of paper and, since he evidently cared enough to wait, what other copy-worthy material was still to follow? However, instead of starting such inquiries, she simply beamed a smile at him through her silver-chained, silver-plated glasses, and said, "Hi," with the open-hearted sympathy of a compatriot of letters. Paper was added, and no questions were asked, but the "Hi" reverberated in his mind because it had the inviting ring of a family gathering to it. That "Hi" was inviting and expectant and somehow Shakespearean in that it seemed to project all persons irrespective of their professions, creeds, or classes—beggars and kings alike—onto the same stage of humanity. On that stage, they might all sit in soft easy chairs by a fireplace and turn pages of voluminous novels, only clearing their throats intermittently to give each other comforting signals of the I'm-here-are-you-also-here? sort. On occasion there would also be the fine tingling sounds of her silver chain. In that world, there was no hunger, no thirst, no itching, just boundless harmony between cerebral and bodily existence.

CHAPTER 2

The Big Bang—matter freeing itself from its timeless existence in singularity, expanding in centrifugal motion, exploding into the new (as yet unheard of) dimensions of time and space—produced gravity and force fields and interactions that reached far out into the cold, empty space, differentiating, clustering into stable states, condensing, condensing, creating conditions for complex systems to form—temporarily, at least—that were able to replicate and pass on their acquired sophistication over generations and to accommodate to the hardships of the emptiness around and the hostility of matter not so organized: living, organic matter—to come finally to the point God was waiting for: slime molds, baker's yeast, white radishes, purple snails, and angora rabbits—and some unknown force pushed some of these temporary organic beings ahead of others, creating humans—violent animals with brains to argue and boss everyone else around—and specifically, after many trials and errors over thousands of years and after many successes at creating non-Huberts, finally created Hubert Belovski, the one who felt the centrifugal pull (a red-shift within himself) every night when he lay awake in his bed made of wood (dead flesh of his green fellow plants!) and listened to the shrill comforting sounds of the cicadas (living flesh of his antennae-bearing sensitive and sentimental fellow souls!).

And in the grand picture that presented itself to Hubert for a fleeting moment, it seemed odd that he didn't spend every living second rejoicing over the unique path of fate that had brought him into existence. Instead, circumstances had forced him to work, and the particular work he had chosen for himself was to study the swirls, funnels, and maelstroms in which nonorganic but nevertheless fellow matter (air and clouds and dust) preferred to move around in the atmosphere.

A cosmic joke?

CHAPTER 3

H ubert drove home in his Corolla after a long day at work. His house stood on the little hill like an ancient castle. This was an absurd idea, considering it was made of wood, colonial style, with the two Doric columns as the only references to a time long past. But the house was stately in some way and had a quietness about it, a solemnity that extended to the trees and the small formal flowerbed in the front and to the unceremonious driveway. The houses next to his were plain, though they were busy with life and the laughter of young children.

It seemed to him he had spent centuries hauling garbage cans back and forth every Monday. There had been a time when the backyard garden, now defunct, had expanded under his hands. It had rewarded him for the love he had invested in zucchinis and tomatoes, but it had also taught him bitter lessons about the cauliflower (mildew-prone and retarded!), the radish (wooden and worm-riddled like antique bed knobs!), and the always unreliable onion.

Every day lately when he returned from work and approached his house, he felt a force clasping him, tightening around his chest. His breathing became shallow as he anticipated the emptiness behind the door. Now, as he opened the door, the way the sound echoed inside the house spoke of the solitude he faced again in the coming night. But as he entered, he saw Sunshine's big brown eyes. They expected him but also mirrored his loneliness. His cat was a solitary, hypochondriac tabby, one of the many possessions Karen had left behind on a November day three years before. Sunshine peed into his boots occasionally, an incorrigible trace of abuse by former owners, but Hubert took these episodes with understanding (*nobody is perfect!*). Besides, his feet produced an odor that could reasonably get a cat confused about the purpose of the two smelly containers.

Sometimes he thought of Sunshine as a permanent witness. Those eyes had calmly watched the scenes of newfound love years ago, when they had chased each other naked through the house from one mirror to the next until they had settled in the downstairs closet for a dusty embrace. The cat had witnessed the times of long breakfasts, with Karen and Hubert draped in Japanese happi coats, reading the *New York Times*, listening to the sounds of the Brandenburg Concerti. Then, three years ago, when the fights started, Sunshine had watched the strange goings-on from a safe distance, as it was her turn to be in the closet, to avoid physical harm.

So, whenever he looked into Sunshine's eyes, Hubert couldn't help reading his own past, curiously distorted through a lens that presumably transformed steaks into mice and Scotch into catnip. There could be some kind of empathy: *Hey, old man, haven't we been through a lot!* But those eyes could also be telling him a nagging *I-told-you-so*. Finally, since Sunshine had seen goings-on before Hubert had come onto the scene, he was tempted to read more: about past lovers and mysterious nocturnal things a cat might have in common with a woman.

Hubert made himself at home. Followed by the tapping of the cat's overlong nails on the hardwood floor, he picked up the mail, walked into the living room, and put his Art Blakey record on. In the kitchen, he opened a can of tuna—how easy it was to keep an animal happy!—and poured himself a gin and tonic. The mail was an assortment of requests for attention and support: Sane Freeze, National Backyard Society, Guns Kill People. Besides, the water bill was there, and a catalog for Macy's intimate apparel. There were new, original misspellings of his name: Belivski, Beloovsky, and—he loved it!—simply Mr. Bell. It was all worth three minutes of attention.

Anticipating the barrenness and anonymity of his mail, he had brought a letter home from work, the day's pleasant surprise. It was addressed to him by a Dr. Schivenhagen from the University of Leiden, in the Netherlands. He unfolded it now to read it again:

Dear Dr. Bolovski:

We are organizing the Twenty-First International Congress on Fluid Dynamics, to be held July 10–15 in The Hague. On behalf of the Scientific Programme Committee, it is my pleasure to invite you to give a presentation on the subject of "The Onset of Critical Conditions in Hydrodynamic Flow." Due to sizable donations from industry, we will be able to pay your registration, hotel accommodation, as well as your economy-class APEX fare. Please let me know at your earliest convenience if you are able to accept this invitation.

I hope to see you in The Hague.

Sincerely,

Dr. Egbert Schivenhagen

Hubert anticipated the trip with excitement. It was less than three months away. Europe was this crammed old world of infinite complexity, a coffee house full of strange foreign voices, full of dissonances, yet, oddly enough, a house where everybody knew his place. In the center of it was the piece of Germany that had been his home, surrounded by well-wishing yet suspicious neighbors. It was still possible to get a rude welcome when speaking German in Holland, and in a way, Hubert felt that by speaking English, he'd enter that country in a masquerade, a wolf in a sheep's clothing, and thereby avoid the unpleasantness stirred up by the past. But he had been less than two years old when the Germans had invaded the Netherlands, and it would be easy to explain that underneath his clothing, there was yet another lamb.

Because there was the other Europe of hope, the increasingly happy intermingling of voices, the sophisticated fabric of urban civilization. There was even the newly relaxed demeanor of custom officers—traditionally, the barking phalanx of national pride. It was this new land he couldn't wait to see again. But there was also the thrill of traveling, of chance encounters, of new possibilities to redefine his life. He watched himself in the mirror for promises that might be written on his face: *Intellectual depth? Affection? Sophistication in lovemaking?* Those were all qualities he claimed to possess. Or was it a face that would cause its bearer to be dismissed as superficial, uninviting, boring, just because of malfunctions in the mechanisms of countenance? He tried out some of his facial muscles and immediately disapproved of what he saw: a strange succession of grins.

The telephone rang; it was his friend Eric.

"Up for a beer?"

"Sure bet."

* * *

Eric, originally among Karen's circle of friends—his nickname was "the Bear"—had stuck to Hubert when the times had gotten tough. He was Irish, blue-eyed and red-haired, with the fierce temperament of his breed, but confined to a wheelchair since the age of twelve due to an accident he refused to discuss. Because of the energy visibly brewing in his friend, Hubert thought of him as an eagle in misfortune, with wings clipped. He lived with his sister in the suburbs.

When Hubert entered The Fountain, he immediately spotted Eric at the round table, half-leaning out of his shiny contraption, finishing his beer. Before him on the table was a yellow plastic bag and another empty mug.

"Hey, what's up," Eric said, giving him the upside-down handshake that had gone out of fashion some time ago. For a moment, the arms of the two friends zigzagged out of sync.

"Nothing much," Hubert said. "Except I got invited."

"Invited where? I hope it's not somewhere in Kansas again."

"Kansas? God, no! No, it's big this time. The Netherlands."

"Lucky bastard! Will you get to see more of Europe?"

"I don't know. Germany, perhaps. And I've got this aunt in Tyrol."

"Tyrol is in…let me guess…Austria?"

"Yes, in Austria. It borders Italy. Up north from there." Hubert turned around to look for the waitress. He signaled her when she appeared two tables farther down. Turning back to Eric, he said, "What's going on with you? Anything new?"

"I'm fine."

"But something is the matter. There's something I see in your face."

"I guess there is. She drives me nuts."

"Who she? Your sister? What happened this time?"

Instead of answering, Eric directed his eyes past Hubert's shoulder.

Lynn, the waitress with the crew cut approached and put her hand affectionately on Hubert's arm. Her lips were painted black, and her face was unusually white. Her mouth looked as if she had eaten charcoal. What was left of her hair was blonde. Hubert, a regular in the bar since his divorce, had followed Lynn's transformation over the years from a country girl to a modish punk; her wonderful lips had been covered first with nothing, then pink, then a bright red, then mahogany before turning into the color of nothingness, of death. What could be next? The visible spectrum was clearly exhausted, and one day soon, her lips might only be visible through an army infrared telescope.

"Hi, Bert! How've you been? Long time no see."

Hubert smiled and gave her a quick tap on her waist with his flat hand. Perhaps it was on account of the synthetic look of her face that he found himself surprised her body still felt warm underneath.

"Hi, Lynn, good to see you," he said. "Two beers, one for the Bear and one for me."

"A beer for Bert and a beer for the Bear," Lynn repeated cheerfully as she headed for the bar. Her voice was always a pleasant surprise: it was the only thing that had not changed.

"Neat girl," Eric said, "despite everything."

"Yeah. A shame, though," Hubert said, sighing. "But back to you. You were saying ...?"

"About Jane. She's got a boyfriend, you know..."

"Your sister has a boyfriend? You never told me that."

"Well, she does. It was never serious before, but now the thing is, they don't have a place to go. He's married."

"You mean she doesn't want to bring him back to her own home?" Hubert said. "I think that's silly."

"That's what I keep telling her. I'm telling her, 'I've got my own bathroom, and we are grownups, for Christ's sake.'"

"But that's her problem, right? What is yours?"

"Well, I think she's resenting the whole deal about living with me. At least, that's what I think is going on. It comes out in all kinds of petty things."

"Like what?"

"Like I have my working stuff in the living room. It takes me ages to get organized each time, so I leave everything out: the accounting sheets, the dictionaries, the manuscript, the books I borrow. Stuff like that. And for her, the whole place is a disaster area, like…she makes it sound like the result of cluster bombing. She says it makes her sick. So, what do I do? Abandon my projects?"

"You know what you need?" Hubert said, leaning toward his friend. "You need some time away from this place. You know, I've been thinking about that. About you. Do you want to meet me in Vienna after the conference? We could do things together. I could push you up the Alps. Seriously!"

"Are you crazy? First of all, think about the cost. Second, you don't know what you'd be getting into. In Europe, you have to travel miles to find a public toilet to fit a wheelchair in."

"We'll get around. And you could get a cheap charter flight. Think about it."

There was an awkward silence. Hubert found himself staring at the bulging plastic bag. "What's in there? I meant to ask you."

Eric opened the bag, imitating the sound of a fanfare, and produced a green thing somewhat bigger than a grapefruit, which he placed in the middle of the table. It was clearly a vegetable but sculpted like a human head. The way it was placed, its green eyes looked firmly at Hubert.

"Aha!" Hubert exclaimed. "The first success with your green monster project?"

"It's going OK," Eric said. "I think I can even start to think about production."

"Holy shit!" The waitress, arriving with the beer, emitted a shriek. "What on earth is that?"

"It's Eric's idea of making money in a big way," Hubert said.

"But it's freaking unreal," she said. "I mean…"

"Ok, I'll tell you," Eric said. "It's simply a gourd grown in a mold."

"They grow on vines," Hubert explained.

"A gourd grown in a mold. A gourd grown in a mold?" she said as she looked up to the ceiling. "You mean you've got some kind of form that makes this veggie take on Lincoln's face?"

"Yup, that's right. Some kind of form," Eric said. "Any face you like."

"Greta Garbo and Elvis as vegetables? Big money? Give me a break!" She laughed as she walked off, shaking her head even more than her hips.

When she was out of hearing range, Eric leaned over toward his friend. "I was going to ask you. Do you have another five grand to invest?"

"Wait a minute," Hubert replied. He suddenly realized that might have been called to the bar for his money, not for his companionship. He quickly dismissed the unsettling idea: friends should be able to make demands without running the risk of such petty accounting.

"Last time you told me you have everything you need," he said. "The seeds, the tiller, a basic set of molds..."

"Rumpelstiltskin, Bambi, Superman, Abe Lincoln," Eric interjected.

"You've got two acres, irrigation pipes, and Stewart. He's still in on it, isn't he?"

"Sure bet," Eric replied. "My *Homo faber*. He'll run it. He knows what he is doing."

"So, what's the five grand for?"

"We need pumps and valves. For the irrigation system. The pumps are run by electric switches, so when everything is rigged up, I can run the whole thing from my desk. Well, more or less. I'll have Stewart only one day a week once things are set up. He's got another job."

"Eric, are you sure this isn't a bottomless pit? I can spare another five grand all right, but I want to be sure I get it back. I want you to be careful."

"Ten back for the five, ten for the other five. It'll work out just fine as I promised, you'll see. No sweat. I showed this thing around. Got everybody excited. I got a letter from the president of the Massachusetts Pet Plant Association. Think about it: combo bands... home decorations... the entire Halloween business..."

Eric interrupted himself as Lynn reappeared and ordered another round of beer. Hubert admired him for his resilience, his humor, his imagination. And there was more; talking with him brought his own problems into perspective: Karen had left him, and before Karen,

Helga, the woman he had once thought he couldn't live without—big deal, there were men such as Eric with no Karens nor Helgas in their lives. Instead, all their mental energy went into maintaining a precarious balance: they needed a powerful fantasy to offset the forces of immobility. The sculpted gourds—fantastic as they were, successful or not as a commercial venture—would contribute to Eric's spiritual survival. In some way, the idea with the gourds was a phallic dream, a dream of swelling, filling, giving life, impressing one's form on unformed substance. By filling the molds, Eric would fill the world with his presence; he would finally overcome the constraints of his condition. Like a tree that produces wind-borne seeds, he'd send out messengers who would travel for him and testify to his ingenuity, strength, and prolific energy wherever they would go.

"What is it doing for you, the conference invitation?" Eric asked, breaking the silence. "I mean, scientifically."

"I don't know. I suppose it's good, I mean, some recognition for me working my ass off."

"Well, isn't this something? You don't seem to be that excited."

This was the question Hubert had been waiting for; he needed someone who would ask this question, and he felt a rush of gratitude toward Eric when he spoke. He started telling him about his feeling of utter insignificance in the library a few hours before, his sense of uselessness in a world where not even his name was unique, not to speak of his role.

"Suppose I dropped dead right now," Hubert said.

"Not here," Eric said. "Don't do that to me."

"No." Hubert protested with his outstretched hand against the intrusion of sarcasm. "I mean, what would be left of me other than the records of my utility bills? Can you think of something?"

"Well, let me think. You showed me some papers you wrote. You were quite proud of those."

"They are by a certain Belovski comma H. That could have been any number of people."

"What about memories of people close to you? Even those who have been close before, at one time or other. Nothing of this is lost."

"Memories! They'll be gone someday," Hubert said, his face cradled between his two hands.

"Listen, on that scale, nothing will be left. One day, only a few hundred million years from now, our sun will expand to the size of the solar system, and every fucking copy of the Britannica will be reduced to ashes."

"You've really cheered me up today. Good try!" Hubert said. "Besides, I have done without the Britannica all my life."

* * *

Back at home, Hubert spent a good part of the night writing in his journal. Sunshine lay curled up next to his chair.

I have spent my life shaking other people's hands. There are all kinds of hands and many kinds of shakes: the ones that melt in your hand like pizza dough, the ones that take on unpredictable errands in circles, spirals, and zigzags, and the kind that is to the point, bringing together firmly the sinews and bones for a cordial moment, but with a movement that carries with it a determination to sever the link as soon as it can be arranged.

The German custom brings hands together promiscuously, incessantly. I shook my father's hand every morning when he came down into the kitchen. I hated greeting one of my best friends because he was elusive in his shake; his hands would change shape, even rearrange bones and flesh, much like the way amoebae crawl, to melt away in my grip even before I could say hi. But it had to be done.

(Customs: habits that go unrecognized, uncommented in the area they rule. One has to leave the Teutonic Reich in order to share the sense of wonder about this constant business of touching.)

Recently, I found out something about the shake, first hand, so to speak. It happened one night when I tried out all kinds of things I might have done once as a toddler. (Why? Being alone makes you ageless; you don't have to profess to the way you look to someone else; you have no role to play; you are little more than a box filled with sensuous memories.) I *licked my knee, pulled one of my big toes toward my forehead, and tried to let my elbows touch each other behind my back. This sounds crazy, but I suppose I was driven by curiosity and challenged by the sheer multitude of possibilities. Perhaps one could call it some sort of workout, except that it didn't require a contraption for $49.99, nor a switch to a new philosophy. Toward the end of my first permutational exercise, when my joints were beginning to hurt and fatigue was setting in, just then, when I was about to stop, my right hand ran playfully into its mirror twin. That is the moment I wish to talk about.*

Each recognized some kind of sameness in the other: touch reciprocated, warmth felt, and the same degree of topological complexity—fingeriness for lack of a better word. Yet there was also an instant feeling of transgression, as in an act of incest. Could it be that the Church, in its long fight for purity, has come up with the idea of folding the hands so as to order and tame the urges of self-exploration? I still don't know this. What I do know is that in the first consciously secular clasping touch of my hands, there was speechlessness, boundless surprise.

What happened next? After a second or so, my right hand remembered that something was missing. It inserted the movement of a shake into the resting pose the way Fellini slips a Bergmann scene into his films: as a jesting quotation, given with a winking eye.

My left hand followed reluctantly, like a woman on the dance floor who doesn't want to be led by the man who courts her, either because she is strong-willed or because she hasn't made up her mind. And in this way, my first handshake with myself developed, my hands embracing each other with the curiosity and shame of lovers in a public square.

CHAPTER 4

Outside, it was dark, cold, and wet, and a mixture of seawater and rain came blasting into Hubert's face as he turned onto the narrow street leading to the hotel. "Aan Zee," said the neon sign in big blue letters. After passing streets with ominous names like *Kolenwagen Slag*, he had worked himself into maritime quarters signaled by *Anker Straat*, Anchor Street, and *Zeeweg*, Seaway. The *Zeeweg* was lit by two yellow lanterns. Along the way to the hotel, he encountered a dog, which took the time to give him a sad, knowing glance. "Aan Zee," he mumbled. "Must mean 'By the Sea.'" And finally, when the *Zeeweg* had reached the *Zeekant*, he spoke in a louder voice to the black mass of the sea that vibrated in front of him in the dark. "Zee," he shouted, "that must be you." Impatiently, without paying attention to him, the sea rolled on.

From the imposing layout of the building and the scale of the neon letters (*My God, do they want the people in Dover to read this sign?*), this surely had once been one of the most prominent hotels on the Dutch seaside. Hubert wondered if Kaiser Wilhelm might have stayed here once, dreaming of war and posterity, tucking his crippled arm under his pillow.

The hotel's interior showed at once that it had seen better days. Everything from the furniture in the reception area to the carpet and the wallpaper had been mended in a peculiar way. The worn carpet, a faded carmine red, bore two orange patches, forever to be eyesores. One of the legs of the mahogany sofa had been replaced by a two-by-four of pinewood that was stained purple. Plastic flowers in the vase had been fixed with tape. Eau de cologne hovered in the air, unsuccessful in camouflaging the stale smell that emanated from the upholstery of the easy chairs. Heavy purple velvet curtains, held with fake gold ropes, gave the foyer a look of faded glory.

The reception desk was a door with a window. (Hubert later found out that the original reception area had been boarded up to house vacuum cleaners, brooms, and buckets.) Posters of bullfights in Barcelona covered the plywood wall. The lower board of the window, the desk proper, was wide enough for a Dutch twenty-five-guilder bill to be passed lengthwise. There was no room for resting an elbow.

As he bent down and looked through the window, he saw an empty room, which shared a door and another window with an adjacent living room. In a last effort to find the receptionist, Hubert stuck his head all the way through the window and looked left and right. He said hello to a gray-haired woman sitting by the wall on the right and knitting forcefully. Upon hearing his voice, she stood up, whipped the yarn out of her way, and focused her glasses in his direction.

"Your name, please," she demanded. Her voice sounded as though she were trying to reprimand him for something. Was it because he was wet? Because he was wearing khaki-colored Navy-surplus weather wear? Or because he had interrupted her needlework?

"Belovski," he said. "Hubert."

"Can you spell that for me?"

"'Be' like 'to be' without the 'to' in front, 'lov' like 'love' without the 'e' at the end, and 'ski' like 'ski' without any change."

"What?" she said, almost crossing her eyes in puzzlement. "Write that down for me." She handed him a piece of paper and a pen.

Her husband emerged from the adjacent salon in slippers and a knitted coat. He was a short, bald man whose face was like a sailor's: crisscrossed by wrinkles and stark red.

"Are you with the congress?" he asked.

"Yes, I am," Hubert said in a patient voice, suppressing his irritation. He had seen enough of the entrance hall to be convinced that all guests of the hotel were there solely because of the congress. Yet that man pretended there actually were people who would seek a room in Aan Zee by their own choice. As he later found out, most of Aan Zee's rooms were, in fact, booked, prepaid in blocks to business people living far away who had no chance to inspect the premises, or to be forewarned, until the very day of their arrival. Hubert remembered the cheerful picture in the flyer: a majestic house with immaculate yellow awnings overlooking the dunes. An elderly man in a black suit and mustache, a charmer of the old school, stood on one of the terraces facing the sea, toasting the waves with a glass of Champagne.

When he finally had the key in his hand, after passing many guilder bills lengthwise over the reception desk, Hubert expected to see his room, number 60, without further delay. Yet the hotel, made up of three connected buildings that had no matching levels, would not allow him to see it until much later. It was not enough that he had paid for the room—he had to *earn it*. His journey was long and complicated, an insult to a traveler who had not slept for a day and a half.

Although the little bald man carried some of his luggage, Hubert's own share was still heavy enough to strain his shoulder. Some of the corridors were exceedingly narrow, and in those, when he tried to change the suitcase from one hand to the other, there was no room for it to turn. Despite all the hardships, there was some reassurance in the touch of the brass key—which he carried in his free hand, and which turned warm as they moved along—that this journey would have a definite end, a terminating point, a certain destination: a place for him to rest eventually.

The spatial relationships among corridors, staircases, doors, and rooms became increasingly confusing; in the course of the journey, he learned to disregard simple clues about the approximate location of his room, clues he had known to hold for hotels of less sophisticated design. When they had gone up one staircase, they would soon go down again, to a level that would be lower than the one they'd started on. Similarly, a long walk toward the south side of the building would suddenly be countered by one going northwards on a different level. Worse than that, there were intervening capricious moves, totally unrelated to the ones before, that dumbfounded his normally keen sense of direction.

His companion, meanwhile, made reassuring grunts and gestures each time Hubert paused and switched hands. Hubert was grateful for his presence, although the physical strain left no chance for a chat. Later on, as the journey progressed and simple common sense demanded some explanation for the extraordinary length of their ascent, the little man's face assumed an apologetic expression, just as the face of a host who asks forgiveness of his guest for the mess left behind by a plumber.

In this manner, they proceeded down three corridors, up and down four staircases, and through one deserted living room and a window-less basement filled with tables and chairs—the *ontbijt* room, where the breakfast would be served between seven and nine every morning. They passed giant sinks and buckets bursting with more bouquets of plastic flowers. A few times, Hubert found himself looking through the window of a locked exit door into the stormy night. Sometimes he ran into a dark image of himself and his bulky baggage in a huge mirror at the end of a hallway. The similarities among these sudden apparitions raised his suspicion that he and his host were making no progress at all, and with a sunken heart, he was preparing himself for the re-appearance of the reception desk and a repetition of the cheerless welcome by the knitting woman.

They reached Number 60 in a sudden turn when Hubert least expected it to happen. The door opened, the little man flung a switch in triumph, and Hubert saw a large room illuminated by a single naked forty-watt bulb. Every so often, the window was lit up by the beam from the light tower. The room smelled of something stale.

"Thank God!" Hubert said, bending down to put his suitcase onto the linoleum floor. ("Ka-lak," it said—the sound of warped linoleum re-joining the floor under the weight of his step.) "It's my room!"

"I wish you a good night," the man said before he turned and quickly disappeared into the dark of the hallway.

Hubert stretched out on the bed and closed his eyes, for once deter-mined to fend off the hotel's intrusions into his well-being. Had he not survived a sandstorm at the Riviera? A night with fleas and worse in Dubrovnik? The attack by a gang of hoodlums in one of Munich's most prominent restaurants? Aan Zee was another reminder of the sad truth that the tendency of the material world was to return to disorder and chaos when left to itself, and that a daily struggle was needed to maintain comfort and dignity against the odds. Against the floods of entropy. And in spite of his present state of fatigue, he decided he was still young and strong enough to stand up to this statistical chimera.

The light blasts coming into the window were uncomfortable, prompting him to inspect the curtains. These were yellow and large-meshed, too short and narrow to fulfill their purpose. The sight of the curtains made him speculate about the diversity in size and shape among the scores of windows scattered throughout this building and its various wings. Originally matched to their host windows, they had been rotated numerous times on their way in and out of the central laundry. His original curtain, the one he might well have encountered in room Number 60 if he had made his entry forty years before (an impossibility; at that time, he'd just been born and would have had to make it to his room by crawling all the way through this exhausting labyrinth), this, his *true* curtain, probably covered the small window of a lucky hotel antipode who, at this very moment, might be stretched out on his bed, unmolested by the flashes of light and unaware of the special nature of his comfort.

The mesh of the curtain cast onto the walls a distorted grid resembling a spider's web, which moved swiftly over the bed, the easy chair, and the silent closet each time the light tower swung its beam across. There was a strong damp odor in the room; to look for its origin, Hubert opened the closet. For a moment, a pungent mildew smell took his breath away. In the closet hung a wet trench coat left behind by his predecessor, who was now probably stumbling, coughing, through the night with the first symptoms of pneumonia. Hubert felt an urge to talk to someone, but all he found (as he said to himself) were the coat and the stale emanations of a stranger.

He fell into a deep sleep. Pictures moved in and out of an encapsulated space that itself traveled with enormous speed. He was a point somewhere in this box, worried about not waking up on time, about the uncertainty of finding his way back the next morning, which he would have to accomplish without the guidance of his host, and about the task of ordering and properly eating his first Dutch breakfast without causing embarrassment.

Then, all at once, in his dream, he was face to face with the wet dog of the afternoon, which was still speechless but now entertained a warm glimmer of affection in its doggy eyes that Hubert did not remember noticing before. The dog's name was Cerb. Cerb smelled like wet dog. It started making curious figures with its tail, and before long, Hubert realized that it was actually trying to convey a message to him. Hubert responded with maritime arm signals, which he had seen in Meyer's Encyclopedia one afternoon in his fourteenth year while scanning the twenty volumes for mentions and pictures of the female anatomy. The pictures of the sailors were engraved in the style of the turn of the century and carried on their faces the imperial pathos of the German monarchy. They were flagging for the good of the German colonies. They were flagging for the *Vaterland*. They were saluting the feeling of pleasure rising in his groin.

All the while, he was aware of the fact that the tail of Cerb, being so close to the dog's pleasure center, was infinitely better suited to express Cerb's gut feelings than Hubert's bloodless arms could ever convey, situated, as they were, in close vicinity to his brain. To an observer, Hubert thought, his movements might look like the fluttering of a scarecrow next to the majestic gestures of an eagle circling in the air.

What added to Hubert's feeling of insufficiency was that the sheer number of alphabetic letters to be flagged made the transmission of even the smallest message a major acrobatic act. He had the suspicion that many fragments might be unreadable to the dog; conversely, there were portions of the dog's speech that were totally unintelligible to him:

Cerb: Me see you on (???) way, 'member?

Hubert: I've been wondering about the meaning of the glance you gave me this afternoon.

Cerb: This house no (???) to animals, dogs, you-likes. Me-dog been chased. Them bury bones, deep, deep. No give them dogs.

Hubert: I could not help but notice some hostility on the part of the concierge.

Cerb: Wanna see some'n? They (???).

Eagerly, Cerb led Hubert to room Number 1, and this time, it was but a small effort to move along the corridors. The door was ajar, and Cerb pushed him gently inside. To this, Hubert objected, but as he was turning around to elaborate his argument, he could not help but cast a glance at the bed in the corner. He saw an old man and an old woman lying side by side, seemingly awake but with their eyes closed. His heart made a sudden jump as he recognized their wrinkled faces. The man was his father and the woman was his mother. They were embracing each other. *They touched each other after all !*—he had suspected it all along!

As he tiptoed backward, he was worried he might step on the dog's wet paws and produce a squelch and a squeal that would wake up the entire house, but then he discovered that the dog was gone without a trace, leaving him stumbling in the cold of the corridor for direction and help. Magically, however, he found a shortcut to his room, which brought him back into his bed in no time. And his bed was still warm.

CHAPTER 5

The morning was misty and the ocean was on the wrong side. But so was the door, and the two walls that were facing Hubert's head and feet. And what was even more remarkable: they all had migrated in the same direction. As he was waking up, hovering uncertainly between inner and outer fog, Hubert discovered that by rotating his bed, exchanging the positions of head and feet, he would be able to restore, for the most part, the familiar arrangement of things. What a miracle to behold! It was worth a few minutes of motionless contemplation. Only his hands were busy, greeting warm, soft, important parts of his body. Hello, hub of Hubert! The only piece of his surroundings that still refused to fall into the pattern of the past night was the sink. Sea and sink were now on different sides of the room, yet he was certain they had shared the same wall only some ten hours before, when the little bald man had opened the door and switched on the light.

He decided to ignore the unpleasant feeling of being betrayed by his memory and give himself entirely to the task of gathering his clothes. "Sea or sink," he mumbled to himself. "Whatever. Sink or sea, what does it matter!"

The smells and light effects of the past night were now supplemented by a variety of sounds, most of them unpleasant, suggesting discomfort of a guest here or malfunctioning of some equipment there. He did not know what he liked less: the moaning and gurgling of aging scientists in the rooms nearby, or the vibrations of a defective shower down the corridor. Intermingled, though, were the sharp, dissonant cries of the seagulls alerted by the early noises of the kitchen. Hubert thought that a place like Aan Zee could not exist without dozens of garbage disposal places; too unlikely, it seemed, that all the refuse would be carried along the uncomfortable path Hubert had been forced to take the evening before. Unless, of course, the personnel shared the secret of the shortcut he had discovered after the wet dog had deserted him last night.

The cries of the seagulls wove a chatty fabric that covered his ears and protected them from the gurgling of the walls. He thought he could make out a distant song:

> *"Sometimes I wonder,*
> *is this all we get*
> *after spending millions of years*
> *growing feathers from scales,*
> *developing beaks,*
> *sharpening the eye?*
> *Look at us now:*
> *we're diving for garbage,*
> *taking trash to the sky!"*

* * *

He found the windowless breakfast room by following the smells of coffee, bacon, and toast. Five tables were occupied with groups of three or four scientists. The white clock on one of the walls showed a quarter to nine. The radio was tuned to a German station that alternated coastal water reports with the early-morning Muzak of Hanseatic department stores. The station faded in and out; the few electromagnetic waves that reached the basement did so only intermittently. This, Hubert knew, was on account of the Heaviside phenomenon; the reflective layer of the atmosphere was adjusting itself to the coming daylight, withdrawing much of its favors from the night listeners, who were now thrown into an exhausting early-morning sleep, the kind that would leave premature wrinkles on their adolescent faces.

He took his seat at an empty table and stared at a blank wall. The wall swam in front of him. It was 3 a.m. on his inner clock, still running on American East Coast time, and he was surprised at the rumbling of his stomach. The few times he'd eaten at this strange hour were when he had been back from a party, drunk, and in need of inert substances such as pickles, cream cheese, and rye bread to encase and neutralize the volatile brew in his stomach.

The conversations sounded subdued, as though the guests were afraid to have their breakfasts taken away. The breakfast, as he could make out from a glance at the nearest table, was made up of an assortment of bread, cheese, and cold cuts served on a platter. Bread, four slices; cheese, three; cold cuts, two. Along with the dish came a cup on a saucer and small can filled with coffee. What he saw was just enough to do a dry run of breakfast, a *Gedankenexperiment* of spatial manipulations.

He could match the slices of bread one by one with the things on top, but that would leave one piece of cheese unaccounted for. Or he could compose generic piles: two pieces of cheese on slice number one, two cold cuts on slice number two. That would leave one true sandwich, containing the remaining piece of cheese between two slices of bread. The true sandwich had an interesting conceptual variant, which would put it in formal equivalence to the series of the generic piles: he could exchange the roles of bread and cheese by putting the two slices of bread on top of the cheese. Finally, he could make one super-duper sandwich using up all the cheese and all the cold cuts on a big pile between two slices of bread and discard the remaining bread, trusting that no food could ever be wasted under the watchful eyes of the seagulls.

The longer he waited, the more the absence of the breakfast on his own table made itself felt. He had exhausted all spatial permutations, at least those that arranged the bread and the cold cuts in a parallel way, like a stack of cards. A man who was chewing and whose cheeks were both stuffed with food pointed him, by means of a fork on which a piece of cheese was stuck, to a button by the door to the kitchen. The very instant he pushed the button, the door opened, and a deep female voice, followed by the large frame of a woman, came out to ask: "Would you like to have breakfast?" Hubert confessed that this was precisely what he had come for. However, when the coffee arrived, he was asked to join another table, apparently for reasons that had to do with some complex scheme of kitchen service consolidation and the careful staging of food delivery in time.

The two guests he was forced to join were engaged in an intense conversation, and he had to deflect his eyes. He did like the European *Boson* habit of social agglomeration, with newcomers joining half-occupied tables, but this morning, filled with flashbacks of his dream, he preferred to indulge in his American persona, which manifested itself in *Fermi*-style exclusiveness.

The conversation stopped, and Hubert found two pairs of eyes staring at him. One pair, which was friendly and slightly magnified by means of rimless glasses, belonged to a Belgian scientist from Loewen, who made an effort to stand up to greet him.

"Sorry," the man said, and it took Hubert a few seconds to realize that Sorry was his name. *Sorry myself,* Hubert had been tempted to say.

"Belovski," he said instead. "Nice to meet you."

The other pair of eyes, which were filled with cold curiosity, belonged to a professor from Dartmouth, who continued sipping his coffee.

"Gilbert. Anthony Gilbert," he finally said.

"I hope the sun is going to make an appearance today," the Belgian man barked in Hubert's direction in a charming Flemish-colored approach to English.

"I would *love* it," Hubert replied. "I got all soaked last night when I arrived."

"Once, in a fog like this, my daughters got lost," Gilbert said. "It took us an hour to find them in the woods. I'll never forget it."

"What were they doing out there?" Hubert politely asked.

"They were five and seven years old then. It feels like yesterday. They found a caterpillar in the brush."

Hubert had seen it before. Accomplished scholars, carrying with them the aura of distinction like an invisible cloak, make odd companions at a breakfast table. One of them might have fresh cuts on his cheeks from a razorblade as blunt as his vision. The second might sport three pieces of fluff on his lapel. The third one might sit there filled with confidence, unaware of the fact that the knot of his tie was seriously misplaced. A threat of imminent disclosure hovered in the air and made their voices rasping and their statements vague.

"There's something on your chin," the professor from Loewen said.

"Thanks," said Hubert, searching with his napkin until he got hold of a crumb of cheese that had stuck to his skin. "I really appreciate it."

CHAPTER 6

*"It may indeed on some occasions be necessary that the Author of nature
display His overruling power in producing appearances out of the
ordinary series of things. "*
—*George Berkeley, from The Principles of Human Knowledge*

Hubert stood crouched in the corner of the shelter at the tram stop, trying to avoid the rain, which came in gushes flying horizontally around corners, straight at him, like the wrath of God. In his hand, he held a red pre-purchased fare ticket, which had turned wet and now clung to his skin like a leech.

The inside of the tram was steaming from wet clothes. He noticed a round, pomegranate-faced woman carrying vegetables in two plastic nets. Three carrots stuck out on the side, still dripping from the rain. The smell of wet fabric was mingled with the scent of a bittersweet Indonesian perfume. The scent brought back the memory of another woman, a memory that had been locked away in a distant corner of his heart: Helga, his fair blond college sweetheart. The sudden rush of images of physical closeness (dancing with her, waking up next to her in the morning) made him wince.

The windows of the tram car were misted. He used the back of his hand to clear a small area in front of his face. Through the curved prismatic strips of water his hand left on the glass, he watched the gray buildings of the unknown city rushing by in curious, wavy motions. He heard small bits of conversation. Some of it sounded German, though distorted and unintelligible, as if the people on the tram were trying to keep a secret from him.

Still damp and steaming, he attended the opening session with the mayor of The Hague on public display, wrapped in his elaborate century-old purple robes. The mayor was an impressive hunk of a man with a bulbous nose, which glowed orange like those of Rembrandt's well-paying clients. Ignoring the international makeup of his audience, he gave his introductory remarks in Dutch. As the guttural sounds filled the big auditorium, Hubert thought about cornfields and vast possessions. When he was a boy, he'd been introduced to Holland through the story of Kannitverstahn, and now the story reshaped itself in his head:

A man is traveling through Holland for the first time. Seeing a large estate—manor, farmhouse, two barns, well-fed cows—he stops his carriage and, lacking even the rudiments of the Dutch language, addresses a stranger in English: "Say, good man, can you tell me who owns these priceless possessions?" "Kannitverstahn"—meaning "can't understand" in Dutch—replies the stranger and walks away. The traveler takes another look at the lands and repeats the word "Kannitverstahn" over and over in admiration. After a few hours, he passes a ripe golden cornfield that stretches to the horizon. Again he halts his horses to speak to the first man he sees on the road, asking him for the name of the person who owns these rolling fields. "Kannitverstahn" again is the answer, and our traveler is in awe, contemplating the immeasurable wealth that fate has heaped upon a single man. As he arrives in the city, his path is crossed by a large funeral possession—scores of elaborately ornamented carriages of noblemen follow the hearse with measured pace. Our man asks one of the bystanders: "Tell me, my dear fellow, who is being honored here—surely, this must have been a man of great standing." Upon hearing the inevitable answer—"Kannitverstahn"—he takes off his hat, shaken by the signs of divine justice: what do all the possessions of good Mr. Kannitverstahn amount to in the face of death?

Scattered applause filled the auditorium; the Dutch address was at its audible end. Whatever the mayor had managed to say about fluid dynamics (the perennial role of the dikes? the roaring elements that his country had to keep at bay?) was lost.

Later, back in the hotel, Hubert spent the evening strolling, exploring entirely new vistas inside wings of the building. In one of the corridors, which had a musty smell, he found gigantic plastic flower arrangements, illuminated by red, blue, and purple spotlights. At the end of another corridor, he ran into a formal vestibule with leather chairs surrounding the giant oil painting of an imposing man. He wore a monocle and the stiff high collar that had been in fashion at the turn of the century. Stepping close to read the plaque that was affixed to the gilded frame, Hubert was amazed to decipher the name of a Dr. Pieter van Zee. Rejecting the idea that the similarity between the names of man and hotel was the result of coincidence, he thought of possible etymological pathways and concluded that van Zee was a contraction of the rigorous but impractical van Aan Zee. Thus, Pieter might have been one of the first guests, who'd gained the right to bear the hotel's name long ago when he'd decided to live here for the rest of his life. Indeed, Hubert thought he could make out a key in Dr. van Zee's well-manicured hand.

Finally, he joined a group of similarly disoriented scientists who silently sat in the lounge watching TV. There, in a live picture from a studio in Luxembourg, a heavyset man wearing blue pants and a red jacket won a two-week vacation trip to the Bahamas for correctly identifying a white velvety flower of the Alps.

"It's *Edelweiss*," he said to roaring applause.

"The trip," the talk master said, with a wink of his eye, "is for two."

A heavy man with a goiter sitting next to Hubert turned toward him. "Any idiot could have done that," he said. "I've never been to the Bahamas."

To which Hubert simply replied with a sigh, "Neither have I." It made him feel good, being part of a conversation.

Outside, the storm and rain continued relentlessly.

* * *

The second day brought a brilliant silence and blue sky. The blue was etheric, pure, the richness of heavens. It was the very tint of blue Hubert imagined when Eric had talked about his longing for a day by the ocean. He found two postcards showing the ocean and the sky in colors that matched those in the real world outside. "Hi," he scribbled on the one addressed to Eric, "things look different here." The other card he was going to send was to his aunt Frieda, who lived in Tyrol. She was from that part of the family that had never left Europe. But in a way, she had moved even farther away from Germany than Hubert: her marriage had brought her to Austria, to her parents' chagrin. Her parents regarded Austria as a caricature of Germany, and Hubert's mother had adopted their views. To his family (though his father had remained somewhat neutral), the dialect Austrians spoke was a sugarcoated kitschy version of the natural language. Vienna was a back room filled with dusty furniture and broken crystal. And of course, Austria's little village Braunau had produced the strangest creature of all, the penniless painter who had led Europe into the abyss.

Hubert had seen Aunt Frieda only twice in his life, and that was when he was still a boy. All he could remember was the high-pitched sound of her voice and the octagonal frames of her glasses. Following a mysterious incident in her life with the Tyrolian husband (an incident that was never explained to Hubert), she had become unmentionable in his parents' house. Even now, after his parents' death, the idea of a visit to Aunt Frieda seemed an act of defiance.

Hubert took the bus, clutching a box with slides in his hands. He was fighting a headache. The Convention Center looked like an architectural drawing, so acute were the shadows of trees and pedestrians in front of its concrete wings. As he walked across the front plaza to the entrance, he saw his own sharply drawn shadow, a strange legless creature that hastened to follow him without delay until it was forced to merge with the mother of all shadows at the entrance to the building.

Hubert's lecture was scheduled for 11 a.m. He approached Lecture Hall Q, where the talk was due.

"Ah, you must be Dr. Bolovski!" a tall gray-haired man said, greeting Hubert with outstretched hands. "I'm Egbert Schivenhagen. I'm so glad you were able to make it. There's a good crowd."

Hubert looked around. The room seated a hundred, but scarcely three rows were filled. He decided to keep his disagreement to himself.

"Glad to meet you," he said.

"Have you been able to see a bit of the city?" Dr. Schivenhagen asked.

"Well, it's been rather wet," Hubert said. "But could you tell me what to do with my slides?" He waved the box in front of the chairman's face.

"Oh, yes, the slides. Lecture Hall P. Take a right and immediately a left. That's where you find a slide carousel."

While Hubert was talking about the onset of critical conditions in hydrodynamic flow and a novel way of approaching the associated closure problem, he noticed that his audience was shrinking. A special luncheon buffet was expected to be served at noon. The applause of the remaining scientists was cordial and polite, but it was clear that their hearts were not in it. Hubert realized that they were already facing the exit door while clapping their hands. There was no discussion, and in fact, there was nobody left to discuss his theories with except Dr. Schivenhagen, who produced a helpless smile. Perhaps the people who attended his lecture would mumble the few comments they might have had into the hors d'oeuvres. His work concerned the formulation of certain turbulence phenomena using chaos theory, which he had to admit was an esoteric subject, but why was there not one person who appreciated the significance of his, Dr. Hubert Belovski's, work?

Depressing as the incident was, Hubert knew his ideas would not be lost; they were neatly sketched out in one of the abstracts of the four-volume Conference Proceedings, whose weight was starting to numb his arms. The afternoon program had nothing of interest. He hurried to leave the concrete complex and walked across the plaza with its waving all-nations flags to take the tram six stops back to the Kurhaus and make his way back to the hotel.

* * *

Hubert sat down on his bed, staring at the low-flying clouds outside for a long time. He felt restless. He had not found a place that could make him feel at ease. He never thought he would admit it to himself, but he missed his cat. His technician had agreed to look after her while he was away. Hubert had left a counted number of cans o'tuna piled up on the kitchen counter and a big bag of litter in the basement. Next to that pile, he'd left the phone number of his vet and a twenty-dollar bill for emergencies. He'd put his stereo on, tuned to WYBX, his favorite station, and left a note:

> *Please leave the stereo on! Sunshine is a sophisticated cat. The music is the least I can do. Could you talk to her once in a while? If you don't know what to talk about, read her from Steppenwolf (the red hardcover on the top shelf in the living room—not the yellow paperback: that's in German!). Start on page 33; she knows it up to there already.*

Now he checked his watch: it was reggae time on WYBX, if he subtracted the six hours' time difference. *What was going on in Sunshine's head right now? Would the beat take some of the feeling of betrayal away?*

The sky and the sea seemed both out of reach and out of scale. The windows could not be opened, and taking the route back along the corridors was a feat he refused to contemplate as he had just arrived— through the endless zigzag tunnel of Aan Zee.

Listlessly he started reading the book he'd brought along, *The Laughing Timberman.* He felt an urge to go to the bathroom. As he put the book aside, he saw a pointed shadow from the corner of his right eye. When he turned his head, there was nothing there but his pair of sneakers, lined up in front of the wall as though determined to march through the brickwork. Then he heard a sharp cry outside. At once, his knees gave in, and his mouth felt dry. He felt shivers running along his back. Had he heard that scream before? It was metallic, not at all human, seemingly bursting with meaning, in a language he could not understand. Where had he heard such a scream before? Perhaps in one of his dreams?

It was then that he heard clicking sounds coming from the window. He saw a white-winged bird fluttering on the outside windowsill, pecking on the glass. Now that he'd noticed it, the bird danced more vigorously—it seemed a dance of beckoning—pointing its beak toward the sea. He could hold his water no longer and went to the bathroom. Relieving himself, he could still hear the nerve-racking sound.

One of those mad birds played an important role in the definition of eternity: There was a bird that came every thousand years to whet its beak on the rocks of a mountain, and when the entire mountain was gone, one second of eternity would have passed. What kind of bird and which mountain were involved in this story was not clear to him, and the way the story used to be told seemed to preclude such petty inquiries. But in fact, the lack of details continued to bother him. The range of possibilities was enormous—at one extreme, he could see a sparrow (or one of the smaller finches) set loose to attack Mount Everest; at the other, he could imagine a stork biting away at the Catskills. Perhaps this was one of the messages of the story: that eternity was so long it did not really matter how you went about measuring it.

When he returned, he found the white little knight jumping at the glass of the window with its full weight, and it sounded as though, at any moment, the pane could burst into pieces. It seemed as though the bird had mistaken his trip to the bathroom as a sign of indifference and subsequently boosted its call for attention. The noise was unpleasant, filling the room up to his ears. *Petty pecking! Bickering beak! Bill be still! Bird, you'll get hurt!* He got up from the bed and put his pants on, closing his zipper in full sight of the crazy finch. With a sigh, he accepted the descent through the maze of the hotel as the price he had to pay in order to escape his beleaguered room.

The beach was waiting for him with a cold breeze but was brilliantly illuminated by the afternoon sun. When he stepped outside, he did not have to look for the bird: it greeted him with pirouettes and long air dives and then settled in a calm corner between two boats just forty yards away from the entrance of the hotel. Hubert walked up to the boats through the fine sand, feeling his heart beat like a man who is dreaming about a radio he cannot turn off. As he approached the spot, the bird flew away, for a moment becoming a stark black shadow only inches from his face. Startled by the sudden movement, he saw light things that had gathered in the space between the boats, caught by the wind: two pigeon feathers, astonishing in their perfection—it seemed they were alive even without a bird attached—a tangle of yellow fishing line, and a crumbled piece of purple paper. The little bird beckoned him from afar, but he stepped closer to the tangle of things between the boats, picked up the flier, and flattened it.

"Fanny Fans! Come to our weekend Dinner Dance" the leaflet said. "Fun, Fun, Real Fun!!!" It was signed by *The Northern Sun.*

Hubert remembered hearing about The Northern Sun, a nudist colony. It was a tale, one of the many rumors circulating inside the hotel about the wonders of the outside world. There were stories about some houses in the *Herengracht,* where girls clad in the loftiest of lace exposed themselves on balconies and actually whistled at the passers-by if they were of the opposite sex. There were stories about a flea market where one could get tattooed all over like the Illustrated Man. And somebody swore he had been to the public toilets in that market and seen a penis decorated with the ten Passions of Christ.

According to the lustful estimate of an aging scientist who had whispered the story across the dinner table, the colony was just two miles east from the hotel, so Hubert figured, considering the strong likelihood of hyperbole, that the distance might be as much as ten—that is, if the place existed at all. Following a sudden jolt of determination, he set out to walk in that direction.

The bird seemed to strongly object to this move: the triumph in its cries, which appeared to celebrate the successful extraction of Hubert from the grasp of the Aan Zee hotel, gave way to a scolding scream, an outburst of anger. Hubert shrugged and snorted through his nose, rejecting any further consultation. If he had to accept that supernatural things existed—and even now, with his body trembling, his mind still rejected that idea—then he preferred to deal with more pleasant manifestations: a black swan singing the love aria from *Aida,* a mermaid in distress who might turn to him for help, or the reappearance of his grandmother to grant him forgiveness for abusing her purple velvet pillow shortly after her death.

When he had imagined himself exploring the nudist colony, he had expected he'd do it on a warm, sunny afternoon. He had seen himself walking along the shore among hundreds of sun lovers, casually, as though with nothing particular in mind except getting from one side of the beach to the other. He'd always been worried that it might cost him a major effort to keep his composure, to keep up that casualness of an innocent mind, because, deep down in his heart, he knew that his true business on this beach would be his desire to breathe in the sight of bare asses, crotches, and breasts and to keep this sight alive and aflame in his body at least as long as the congress lasted.

His visit to the nudists' beach turned out to be quite different. The weather had left only those roaming around outside who felt adequately dressed by calluses and goose pimples. These were the professional nudists who had burned their clothes back in '68 in a midsummer bonfire, the very fire that had consumed many of the finest brassieres. These were the kind of nudists that would have been attractive to him only with their clothes *on,* which they wore, as they admitted, in their private homes, where they had to face such non-nudist tasks as letting the gas meter man in to meter their gas.

"Helga!" he shouted. He waved his arms at a woman close to the edge of the beach. It had to be her from the way she walked.

"David?" she shouted back, running toward him but then stopping abruptly. "Oh, it's you, Hubert. Oh good God, Hubert, it's you!"

She took a few more steps, bringing her nipples into his focus. They were hard, blue, and stiff. *God help me!* Her pubic hair was a fine brush, with speckles of sand hidden in it that glittered in the evening sun.

"What on earth brings you here?" they exclaimed almost in unison as they both took a final step to embrace each other.

"I'm Einstein on the beach," he laughed. She had called him Einstein once, alluding to his—as she believed—foremost cerebral existence. "How've you been? What happened to your Kraut?"

"Turned sour long time ago," she replied. "Where did your ballerina go?"

"Danced all the way to the moon," he said, putting his hands on her shoulders and waist as in a slow waltz. One of his hands slipped, and he suddenly remembered his vow to stay away from women with flat buttocks.

But it was too late. A complicated chemical reaction had again started in his body. "This morning, for some reason, I was thinking of you."

"You. Were. Not!" Helga said with mock reproach. She smiled back at him as she had always done: her eyes squinting, her head slightly reclined. Her blond hair was much shorter now. Her buttocks? They were flatter, too.

"You are right; I was probably not. But I was pretty close to it. I've been having a headache all day, and I remembered what you would do to make it go away."

"Like what? What would I do?" Helga asked. She had taken a step back to eye him fully. Her arms were folded in front of her chest, forming a sturdy couch for her breasts. They had changed somehow, but again, how could he tell? She stood on one leg, angling away and stretching the other so that the big toe, barely touching the sand, left the trace of an arc.

"Remember the stuff with the aurora?" he said, watching her, imagining a bikini on her. "Aurora is all you talked about. That the energy in your body is quantized. That you had to be careful to keep an odd or even number of quanta in your body depending on whether you were of the *lapis* or the *lazuli* kind. That lapis and lazuli were the yin and yang parts of the aurora. At least, sort of." He felt stiff, almost inadequate, next to her.

"I wished you had forgotten that crap," she interrupted him curtly. "I think it's pretty boring. Actually, it's exactly as boring as you once told me it was."

It was clear she resented that he had brought up the subject of a conversation that had marked the end of their relationship. And for him, that resentment spelled out hope. In an attempt to keep up the spirit of the occasion, of a miraculous reunion years away from a glorious summer in Munich, he exclaimed: "It's *so* good to see you! How have you *been*?" with a high-pitched sound of "been."

"I don't know. Pretty good, I guess. Getting on." The tone in her voice had a trace of hurt, and of reluctance to be so readily appeased.

He suddenly remembered the feeling of her breasts pressing against his body; it seemed as if all the way, through sweater and shirt, they had left two burning marks on his chest. He decided not to tell her that he still missed her sometimes.

Hubert used the pause to glance down over his sweater and pants for traces of sand at the approximate positions where nipples and the magic triangle had intersected the fabric. He was careful not to brush off the little he could find.

"Who is this guy David?" he asked.

"What David?" she said.

"From a distance, you called me 'David' at first." Hubert started feeling silly about asking.

"Oh, that David. He's just ... some nice guy."

CHAPTER 7

"Two physical 'points'—a mark, say, on the measuring-rod, and another on a body to be measured—can at best be brought into close proximity; they cannot coincide, that is, coalesce into one point."
—Karl R. Popper, from The Logic of Scientific Discovery

Obscene separation of our bodies! Yearning of the soul makes the flesh burn, moves bodies towards each other into a singular song. But what do they do with Siamese twins? Cut them apart! Here are a few humans who have been endowed with the unity others strive to achieve. Can you believe what do they do to them? Cut them apart!

Who is Helga? A friend. What else? A friend with fine, silky skin, beardless, and otherwise just like you. Everything is almost exactly like you. Except for a silly detail, a thing that is no more than an idea. A minuscule negative nothingness, an obsessive idea, an idea that has more than its proper share among all ideas swirling around in your head. Helga is a fine friend with beautiful hair. But she is also a complement, her body to your body, her yearning to your yearning, occupying a place in mankind's striving for unity that was once obscenely broken.

* * *

"Remember me?" Hubert said to Helga, touching her hand and then clasping it firmly with his two hands when he discovered how cold her skin was.

"Yes, I do remember you," she replied cheerfully, looking into his eyes.

"What are you doing here?" he asked.

"Vacationing. I joined the *Northern Sun.*"

"Good for you!" he said. "I read this funny flier about a dinner dance.

But what on earth is this place? I thought it's just a fenced-in area for people without clothes."

"Everything here belongs to it," she said, gesturing with her free hand, pointing to a group of cabins arranged around a wooden building and a deck with plastic chairs and a huge blue flag that said "NIVEA" in white letters. Then, with a sweeping motion, her arm claimed all of the sea up to the sharp line of the water on the horizon, from south to north. "You know *Club Méditerranée*? Same idea. We even get to live on the beach."

"Must be some club," he murmured, letting go of her hand, which he had brought back to an acceptable temperature. Helga's gesture had carelessly included the very place that was his present life support, Aan Zee, certainly no subsidiary to a nudist club, but rather a self-contained, proud establishment in its own right; despite its deficiencies, it was the very negation of bareness. Inside the hotel, he had been reluctant to say a good word about it. A single word of praise might make the butter disappear from next morning's breakfast table. Yet outside the hotel, he felt an odd urge to defend that little world.

He suddenly realized that it was not just the violation of privacy he was reacting to; it was the encroachment of a nudist club in particular that was an offensive thought. He was disturbed about the idea of seeing the hotel manager and his knitting wife walking through the corridors of Aan Zee without attire. There were certain guests he would not even have liked to see without a tie. And perhaps it was also the thought of strangers watching the embrace he had seen in his dream that made him cringe.

Unsure about his feelings after this intrusion, he glanced at her from the side. Once she had been his princess; he remembered her alabaster skin, the grace of her movements. Now her body was goose-pimpled and blue, mercilessly displayed against the ocher color of the late-afternoon sky. And the movement of her hand that had staked claim to much of the visible coast had been plain careless, without control. *Northern Sun, what kind of crazy sun is that?*

She motioned him toward a row of wooden cabins standing in the distance, just where the beach bordered the elevated road. They came in all colors of the rainbow, but the colors were jumbled, not quite in order, just as the trees back home in the Berkshires were on a clear September day.

Next to the row of cabins was a volleyball field, still busy with two undressed figures (*wobbling pointed profiles against the sky!*) and a fast-moving, flesh-colored ball.

"The blue one with the yellow door," she said. "I get real cold as soon as I stop jogging."

Yes, jog she would. He could have thought of that. The Helga he had dated back in college would have jinked if jinking had come into fashion, and jink she would in a jinker's outfit. That merciless timeliness! That deadly accuracy of cultural ambience! She was one of those people who dwelled in the armpits of the zeitgeist. This thought created a little disturbance, just enough for his foot to pause when he directed his steps toward the blue cabin with the yellow door.

He felt he had acquired another stage of maturity in all these years; *just* let *me handle this,* he was telling his timid self when it trembled facing Helga again, and with her the renewed possibility of pain. Yet there was another voice that whispered into his ear. *Stay out of this!* it said. *There must've been a reason to split up then. How can you be so sure things are so different now?*—*Shut up,* he said sharply, and at once, there was a chorus of acclamation by other parts of his body: *Shut up, shut up, shut up!* they hollered. *You goddamn fool! How silly to think about the future! We're talking a few days max!* With that, his foot proceeded with its movement toward the yellow door.

The small cabin was warm and smelled of salt and sun lotion. The fine white sand was everywhere (this was the place to brush it off from his sweater!). Bundles of clothes were scattered on the floor, mostly of the delicacy, size, and coloration that suggested female ownership. There were salmon-colored silk undergarments, which lay doubled over in wavy patterns like the northern lights. A long patchwork skirt had been draped over a rocking chair, facing the window as if still waiting for the owner to arrive and break the spell that had brought this early abandonment. Fluffy blouses lay there, formless and in disarray, in the accusing gesture of curtains separated from their windows.

In the middle of the room stood a large, sweetly unmade bed, from which linen and pillows cascaded toward the floor. Hubert imagined conversations among pieces of clothes once worn and now neglected by nudists. Pathetic outcries, whimpering sobs, attempts to recall happier times when they had been part of a functioning wardrobe, either neatly layered and folded, and waiting for their outing, or on their way somewhere in the orderly procession of wash, spin, dry, iron, and wear.

Some of the clothes belonged to a man; this grave fact could not be overlooked, and Hubert did not like the sight of it. There was a pair of socks so large and dreadfully colored Helga would not have worn them in a thousand years. Without moving his head, Hubert quickly glanced through two doors into small adjacent rooms to check for traces of other inhabitants, in-sleepers, in-laws, co-nudists, or, as he now had to admit to himself, competitors. The check was inconclusive.

Yet there was something in the way she offered him coffee that assured him there was no other person in the cabin, and the very moment he realized this, the descending cascades of linen suddenly appeared to reverse their direction and ascend instead, from the floor to the bed, in a graceful gesture of invitation.

Once in the cabin, she had put her jeans and T-shirt on, following the reversed domestic habits Hubert thought common among nudists. And what happened then was that the packaged parts of her body at once regained the sheen only male imagination can provide by a process of extrapolation that works on the subtlest of clues. Sometimes it is the sinew of a woman's wrist, just where it emerges from her sleeve, that conjures up the smoothness and firmness of her whole body. Hubert was reminded of Goethe's struggle to link the shape of a plant's leaf to the way it bloomed. *There's no limit to a mind that is on fire.*

They took coffee and Dutch pastry in Roman style, lying on the bed, elbows resting on the mattress. They both had their heads cradled in their hands, facing each other across a small tray as little clouds of steam rose from the hot cups. Eating the pastry made their heads go up and down, and in order to stay level, they discovered, they had to chew in exact synchrony.

Hubert told her about the hotel and its odd regimen. Whenever he had thought about running into her again, he had imagined an epic outpour, a breathless recounting of the things that had happened in the interim. But of course, it now occurred to him, minds don't work that way; minds always work backward. He had to talk about the closest thing in the past and then watch out for tunnels, wormholes that would lead further back, and hope she would have the courage, patience, and imagination to follow.

"You know, in a way, it brings up my childhood," he said. "Every moment I spend at this place, I feel like running away. But I also feel like I belong there. Isn't that strange?"

Helga talked about the ways of her colony. There was a walk-in cinema, a fenced-in area of the beach where you could stretch out in one of those folding chairs, eat your ice-cream, and watch a giant screen. They showed movies about *Freikörperkultur*—the culture of the free body—as practiced on the beaches of Madagascar and Rhodes. She had seen a documentary about a day in the life of an aboriginal tribe in New Guinea.

"It's all real natural. We're just spending our time here without hang-ups. That's all there is to it," she said.

"What do you do with someone who gets an erection?" Hubert asked. "I always wanted to know."

"It doesn't happen," Helga said, frowning.

"Come on. I find that hard to believe. This afternoon, when I was walking along the beach, I was thinking how fortunate I was to have my clothes on," Hubert said, patting one of the legs of his pants as if to commend it for its good manners, like a faithful dog.

"Well, there was this one incident, this swine," Helga said, spreading her hand out, which made Hubert wonder if she were singling out one of her fingers for mimicry. "They had to throw him out."

"The men here must be pretty old, then, in the colony?" Hubert said. "I mean… You know what I mean."

"I guess you're right. I never thought of that," Helga said, laughing.

"Anyway, I'm glad you joined the Northern Sun," Hubert said. "Because that the flyer about that club was the only reason I walked all the way over here. I would never have run into you just commuting back and forth between conference and hotel."

Hubert mused about the fate that had made Helga choose Scheveningen, of all places, to spend her vacation at the precise time when the Fluid Dynamics Conference was to be held. It turned out that there was a friend of a friend of hers who had suggested this place for Nudists or *Nackedeis*. Neither was a scientist, so it was sheer unblemished coincidence. Helga remembered the time when they were flying kites, and did he still have the one with the Marco Polo face?

In that way, stories begot others as swiftly as rabbits beget rabbits, until they filled the cabin like a furry mass from wall to wall. Hubert had the feeling that they had reached the point again, like in their hey-days, when their curiosity about each other was boundless: Helga would not rest until she knew where he had bought his weathered shoes, and he would likewise study her face for signs of the time that had passed. There was thus the promise of many days to come that they might spend in similar ways: in wonder, in recognition, in recounting.

The comfort of lying on the bed—still seal-like belly-down supported on elbows—the warmth of the air, and the pleasant rush of blood stirred up by the coffee, all that filled him with unrestrained joy.

"I still can't believe this. How did it happen?" he asked.

"We ran into each other," she said. "And that was the part of fate. But from that moment on, we've been in control."

"Control. Yes," he said, stroking her head, which seemed so close and yet so distant still.

Then after they had run out of things to tell in this first spate of tell-ing, Hubert tried to imitate the scream of the bird he thought was the ultimate sponsor of the sudden bliss, until Helga asked him to *please, please stop*, would he? A little later, without rush and without a prompt-ing signal, they both took their heads out of their hands, straightened their elbows to regain full control of their arms, which were about to get numb, sent the tray with its empty cups down the stream of linen toward the floor, and embraced each other.

* * *

God's secret! God's secret secretion! God's secret Bavarian brass band!
   Where is the eternal fountain?
   I forgot. I will never forgive myself if I have lost it forever!
   It's right here, my darling. Don't worry. It has always been here for you.
Where's your plummet?
   Following the pull of gravity!
   Blessed be gravity. Sound my well! Dive into the fountain
   The fountain of hope? Of forgetfulness?
   Of forgive-you-ness, of forget-me-never-again!
   Foreskin saga! Kind kindling of foreplay
   Hansel forlorn in the forest of Gretel

* * *

There he stood again, naked, in the circle of light emitted by a light bulb that hung from the ceiling of his parents' bathroom; the light cast a shadow from top to toe, creating a dark, two-dimensional homunculus hovering around his feet. It had a giant, warty head with the shadow of Hub's nose for a nose, the shadow of his ass for a skull, no eye for an eye and no tooth for a tooth.

Now the light that had been above him had magically descended and had become flesh that was about to open up, still swirling around in a slight singing motion. There were again the voices belonging to his parents and his elder siblings in the dining room next door, speculating what might one day become of him. *Nothing,* he had thought at the time, *absolutely nothing!* And after a short while of watching homunculus' grimaces, he'd added: *Of course, they don't know, do they, that I masturbate every night and that in a few years, my spine will be gone, leaving the rest of my body vegetating. In an asylum.*

Just then, the last segment of his spine was catapulted into the warm fountain above, defying gravity as it were, and he died, and that was that, and it did not seem to matter. But when he tried to open his eyes, they opened just as before, and those sweet nipples were still in place, looking at him firmly without recognizing him—*a blind date!*—as they continued their parallel zigzag dance, which was slightly out of phase, marking a local disturbance in the universe. He thought about all those other breasts that were now in similar motion—the sun was setting, and surely, many lovers were celebrating, in similar constellations, the brilliant day that had passed. *The moment when all those breasts would cease to move, that would be the end of love, the end of turbulence, the end of physics, and the end of the world he truly cared about.*

CHAPTER 8

"To say we see 'everything' can no longer be much of an exaggeration"
—Nigel Calder, from Violent Universe

T rees were flying by; the tram followed the beeline of the *Scheveningse weg* and was occasionally struck by a low branch, which produced a denotating sound. Hubert addressed the other people on the tram in his mind: *And above all, my fellow travelers on your imitation leather seats; above everything else, you must know that Helga loves me. Helga loves a man, and by a wonderful coincidence, that man happens to be me!* He wanted to chant his lover's chant into the world, which still went on in its tracks as if nothing had happened. *The years of estrangement were over forever: what a terrible misunderstanding this had been! Yet all along, fate had meant them to be together, and fate had succeeded in the end.*

When had they met the first time? Fifteen years ago? On a bus, of course, how could he have forgotten that! It had been a bus with green plastic-covered seats. The door had been jammed and when he'd forced it open from the inside with a jerky movement of his arm, that girl had firmly fallen into the bus with an astonished cry; what had made her cry was the sudden pain and the swiftness of the force jolting her. The look of surprise on her face did not go away when the excitement about the door and Hubert's move subsided. There were bruises on her shin; there was blood. That was the first time he had touched her leg.

The tram, as though conspiring with his yearning mind, passed a bakery to remind him of the pastry on the unmade bed the day before. It then stopped in front of a pharmacy that had the light-blue NIVEA sign prominently displayed. A little later, Helga's sunglasses entered the tram, riding the nose of an otherwise undistinguished girl, and the sight of the purplish tint brought back the reflections of the wide horizon on the beach and the small world they had shared afterwards. Closing his eyes, he could still feel the touch of her skin. My cells remember, he said to himself. How many have I got? Must be billions, trillions. And each and every one of them sings the same song!

In this jubilant way, he missed his stop. The buildings along his way looked quite unfamiliar, and at the first chance, he got off the tram in a haste. *This never happens to me. It's just that…my mind must be somewhere else.* And as he set out to trace his way back, he noticed with satisfaction that it had started raining. He enjoyed the fine touch of the droplets on his skin, the tickling when they hit his eyebrows, the caress by the tiny streams of water running down his cheek. The rain quickly turned into a downpour. He stayed close to the trees for shelter. In the gutter next to the sidewalk the water passed in large quantities, rippling and gurgling, happily accepting its final destination: the Northern Sea.

Being alive, what a wonderful feeling that is! He could have kissed a yellow traffic sign just because of its unabashed yellowness in the rain; he felt the touch of his own warm hands, buried as they were in the pockets of his coat, on his own hips through two layers of fabric. Now each step toward the Conference Center was part of a circle that linked it with Aan Zee and Helga's current domicile. Each step was a joyful event, for it brought him closer to her cabin and the bliss awaiting him within. Being alive, that meant moving in the magic circle, and circles—that much was known and celebrated throughout the ages—had no end.

"Critical Phenomena and the Onset of Turbulence in Viscous Media: Room F, on the East Gallery," the blackboard said in the entrance hall of the Conference Center. Or should he go and listen to a hydrodynamic model of the traffic flow on the Place de la Concorde? That would be Meeting Room W, next to the cafeteria, in the opposite direction. *(He would show her Paris, yes! "Here are two tickets to Paris," he would simply say. "Let's go!" And once in Paris, and headed for the Champs-Élysées, he would tell her: "this here is the Place de la Concorde. I even know how the traffic flows.")*

He decided to go for the hydrodynamic lecture because of its vicinity to a place where he could get coffee and because its topic carried promise for an adventure in the near future. He joined the line for coffee. After a while, the man in front of Hubert turned around and said, "Hi." Hubert answered his greeting with a perplexed expression; he firmly felt the muscles in his cheeks stiffen. The man's face was so close that Hubert saw the pores in his nose and the red capillaries in his eyes. Hubert tried in vain to increase the distance, but the line behind him was unwilling to budge. The last time a face had been so close to his, it had belonged to Helga. What a world lay between those faces! What a wide range of phenotypes existed in the human race!

"You don't remember me?" the man said. "We met at the breakfast table. Remember the butter lumps with the seagull relief?"

"God, I'm so bad with names," Hubert said. "Yes, you were the organic chemist…"

"Inorganic. Chemist is correct."

"Inorganic chemist, yes. And you had these two teenage boys who got lost in the Rockies once…" Hubert said.

"In the Adirondacks. And girls they are. But you got the basic idea right," the man said. "And by the way, my name is Gilbert. Anthony Gilbert."

"Hubert Belovski. So glad to meet you again," Hubert said and shook his hand with a nod. "How do you like the conference so far?"

"I'm glad I came. My interest, I might have told you this morning, is in the history of the chaotic theory of turbulence. And by a stroke of luck, two old-timers are here. I'm doing oral history with them. To get them going, I took them to a bar in the Old Town. They are quite disorganized, I should have known."

"Disorganized? How so?"

"Scattered. Forget where their wallets are. That sort of thing. Forget what they are doing here. There's Miller, you know, the Miller of Miller et al., 1961, and he tells me how he used to do his computations on a machine that worked with valves, filled a whole room and got steaming hot. And there's Boistenhain, who used to be Miller's worst enemy— and it's still quite a job to get them to sit at the same table. So, this Boistenhain, out of the blue…"

"Black or white?" the woman at the counter asked as she was filling the cup with coffee. She was dressed up in a traditional Dutch costume, which brought out the nicest parts. She was sort of pretty. *Helga's got a soul*, Hubert quickly corrected himself. *This one just has the looks.*

"White, with cream," Gilbert said. "And this Boistenhain—he is German, you know—starts telling me the story with the cows…"

"What about sugar?" the waitress said. *(She does have a sweet accent, though. But how she pales beside my lover!)*

"What about it?" Gilbert said. "Just leave it out! Where were we? Yes. Someone asked him, 'What do you do?' and he said, 'I study cows…'"

"Excuse me," Hubert said, "it was nice meeting you again, but I've got to hurry. I'm headed for the Place de la Concorde."

"Boistenhain," he mumbled when he was a safe distance away. *Miller et al.! Cows! Enemies! Romans! Countrymen! Who cares about their oral history! Valves! Steam! His nephews lost in the Alps! The history of chaos is chaotic, like all of history. That much we know without getting old scientists loaded in a bar. Helga will love this story. I will love her loving this story. She will love me loving her loving this story. Being alive in a circle: The traffic on the Place de la Concorde. Con-corde: two hearts beating in unison. We're already there!*

CHAPTER 9—HELGA

She swam with long strokes in the calm early-morning sea. The water was cold beyond pain. Her head was like a vessel, looking ahead to breathe in the light and the air. She was alone, celebrating the absence of demands, the absence of daily struggles, by yielding all of her skin to the water. It touched her as no man would; her neck, breasts, loins were whipped by a thousand cold hands, but they were also stroking, kneading, cleansing, knowing.

It was an act of sheer madness that had made her decide to spend her vacation alone in a nudist club; it seemed hard to come up with a place where she could be less protected, more at the mercy of strangers. Yet, in an odd way, she felt quite safe. In the colony, there was a detailed accounting of everyone's actions; just as the sun duplicated the hairs on her skin without fail, giving each a silent companion, so it watched over the orbits of the citizens of her newfound world. The hand of a man that moved to transgress would, in the process of moving, be halted by a burst of light and by the eyes of people who *saw*. Every hand of every man knew the Law of the Light and stayed put. The nights were different, no longer ruled by light, but instead, the colony was transformed into a place governed by the rules of socialites with silk gowns and fine Cashmere wool suits.

This was her first vacation spent alone, without her boyfriend. They had planned to go to Barbados; they had already bought the tickets and spent time talking about what it would be like to sleep in the stylized grass hut by the beach that came with the deal. It was to be the place that would make up for the daily erosion of faith in a common future. And then, one day at breakfast, something funny happened. It was something she still could not understand. He'd lifted his arm and scratched his temple the way he always did, closing his eyes, and she'd been unable to see herself having one more breakfast with that man.

A scattered swarm of seagulls lifted off with sharp cries above her head, flying toward a sparkling point in front of her on the horizon: the first excursion boat, packed with tourists whose pockets were filled with yesterday's bread. Probably the harbor trip: two hours, five guilders; kids under six, two and a half. Her skin was numb now, and her body, ceding its chilled outer shell to the ocean, felt strangely lukewarm; in that state, the cold could creep through her subcutaneous layers and catch her muscles unawares.

She turned around without haste. Before her now was the spectacle of the coastline; the orange sun was rising behind a ragged blue-grey ribbon. A streak of golden reflections, alternating with large circles the color of anthracite, ran across the water toward her, connecting her with the new light of the day. One of the buildings was Aan Zee, she suddenly remembered, mysterious abode of Hubert, who had suddenly walked into her refuge, carrying with him the past like a weapon. There was only one way she could deal with a man: as a single cosmic event followed by silence that allowed her to listen to waves of remembrances and fantasies. He had bought tickets for a theater performance the coming night. "Just come in the afternoon," she had said good-humoredly. "I'll cook something. And then we'll go out." His face had lit up like that of a little boy seeing the first Christmas tree of the season. She was free like the waves, like the fish, yet something was closing in on her: the net of a man's expectations. She knew Hubert. He would set into motion every device of his intellect, every routine and subroutine of the Big Program stored up there, to go through the sequence of the past night again. That part of love was an addiction of the worst sort, and apprehensively, she had to face the curious role of being a drug dealer, helpless therapist, and withdrawal cure all at once.

A thought interfered with her steady movements. *What in the world did he eat? Chicken or beef?* She had vague memories about a dinner with the Hubert of the old times in a steakhouse. But a lot might have changed. Just two weeks before her departure, her girlfriend from college had turned Buddhist. Helga was certain about one thing: that he had not turned vegetarian. *All vegetarians she knew spent a good deal of time talking about food. He didn't. So, it was chicken or beef. Somehow he came across as softer, less macho than last time. Chicken then.* This intuition had a calming effect, just for a second. But then, *what if she was wrong? What if he detested chicken?* She focused on the big NIVEA sign, the mark of the Colony, and steered in its direction. *No cramps now—they would spoil everything.* She tried to do her strokes evenly, and in her mind, there was a voice that sang in synchrony: *Chik-ken—or beef. Chik-ken—or beef? She would try to call him at the hotel. No—to do that was too domestic; he would resent making a choice ahead of time. And it would be too…blunt, too un-casual, too uncool, making her look too invested at this early point. Chicken, then. If he liked it, she'd* say, "I knew you would!" *If he didn't:* "Listen, buddy, I had to take a chance!"

* * *

The phone rang. It was bright outside. *Why…was she asleep?* She found herself wrapped in a large beach towel right in the middle of her large bed. She remembered her skin hurting like fire in the shower and her heart racing like a deer when she rested afterward. She remembered the slits of the blinds brightly lit by the sun, a pattern that continued to burn when she closed her eyes. The voice of a woman asking for her:

"My name is van Wedelen. Adele van Wedelen. I'm calling about your note on the bulletin board." A formal, British tone. The correctness of this voice was so at odds with the state of her surroundings that Helga felt compelled to straighten her hair and turn with the receiver toward the only one smooth corner of her bed.

"Bulletin board? Excuse me, I'm just waking up. Oh yes, that…note."

"Your note about bridge in the Kurhaus. I understand you are looking for partners. I'm game, excuse the pun. I'd love to play. We arrived three days ago. My husband is here on business for a few days, and I'm left to my own devices."

Devices? What is she talking about? Knitting needles? Crutches? Telephones? Bicycles? Folding chairs? Vibrators? Helga tried to gauge the woman's age from her voice, but there was no trace of brittleness: this was the full voice of a matron whose daughters had just left for college and who was now furiously determined to enjoy herself. But what misfortune! Her companion was probably tied up in an office of business partners in the center of The Hague. Surely a tedious deal, only occasionally interrupted by a heavy lunch of *Rijstaafel* in one of the restaurants named *des Indes.* By now, on the third day of her stay, she would have done the Scheveningen beach promenade a good dozen times. She would have walked across the Circus Plaza, past the columns of the Circus Theater, glanced into the Nautical Museum, and discovered the three local art galleries. Unable to focus on the eclectic kind of art that had originated during her own lifetime, she would have rushed on to the five absolutely charming local boutiques. It was here where the woman who belonged to that voice would have discovered the true torments of time and solitude: she had nobody to talk to about the beauty of things on the shelves, like the fine high-necked porcelain cat and the batik shawl from Guam.

For Helga, Bridge was a casual amusement but listening to that accurate, singing voice on the phone, she sensed that for this woman, Bridge could be part of a scaffold for an oppressive life.

"Sure," Helga said. "I know what you mean. This place is no Paris. There's little to do. I'm so happy you called. I've got to kill time for a different reason. But Bridge … Bridge absolutely fascinates me."

The woman at the other end was quick to point out that she and her husband were staying at the Kurhaus Hotel, the one that many years ago had surpassed Aan Zee in prominence and elegance. The Kurhaus Hotel was so close to the Northern Sun that Helga thought she had to ask her new bridge partner to stop by for *Thee met gebak*—tea with cookies—in the afternoon. "Just for a little while," she said, "because of a later engagement."

* * *

Adele van Wedelen arrived at Helga's cabin at four on the dot. The chicken casserole was in the oven (*sorry, Hubert, too late for beef!*), and the salad was already made, now waiting in the fridge in a plastic dish, beneath a taut film of cellophane. Helga's guest was a woman barely five feet tall. She wore a straw hat with a yellow ribbon, and more yellow to follow on her small body: an egg-yolk colored blouse (*how practical at breakfast!*), a white skirt with a meandering bright-yellow seam, and shoes that looked like walking buttercups. The abundance of this difficult color made her skin look like parchment from the Dead Sea scrolls; whoever her husband was, he had to have some serious kind of blindness to go on living next to this artificial sun.

It took Helga some time to make out Mrs. Wedelen's face and her hearty, good-natured smile.

"Step in!" Helga said. "I'm so glad you came."

CHAPTER 10

"Wherever we are, what we hear is mostly noise. When we ignore it, it disturbs us. When we listen to it, we find it fascinating."
—John Cage, from The Future of Music: Credo

Hubert slept long, and the minute he got up, there was a whistle on his lips. He whistled his way through the shower, through the ritual of shaving, of selecting a shirt. He whistled at himself in the mirror and approved his appearance: a face that was vibrant with confidence and desire. He started with the tune of his favorite line in Carmen, "No woman/before you/has so deeply/stirred my heart," and ended with one of the scenes of lovers' confusion in Don Giovanni just before he brushed his teeth. It was eleven o'clock, which left plenty of time for a hearty breakfast someplace outside Aan Zee, a stroll to the liquor store where he would pick up a bottle of crème de menthe, and many unscheduled yet welcome interruptions by strangers on his way. On the way out the door, he stopped himself: time for yet one more chore, a postcard to Eric. It had to be done now since tomorrow would be Saturday and on Saturdays the post office closed at noon.

Dear Eric:

Greetings from the Netherworld! I wished I could take you to one of the bars. The conference is OK except for the lectures. Remember Helga, my girlfriend from college? I mentioned her name to you a few times. We literally ran into each other on the beach, and it felt as if no time had passed. Superstitious as I am, I better stop my account here.

Eric, do me a favor: next time you're in the Fountain, drink to me and my newfound, newly-recovered love. Wish me luck! I can use it.

Best wishes,

Hubert

P.S. When you write to me, don't forget to tell me about your green friends!

There was a mild breeze outside, coming from the sea and carrying the smell of salt and seaweed. The sky had just recovered from the onslaught of morning pink, and had assumed a noncommittal light shade of blue. He watched a regatta of five clouds drift across the firmament and saw the ensuing ecstasy of victory: the cloud that won split into two at the precise moment it touched the horizon. What a perfect day to take a girl out to a play!

But he had barely gone two blocks when he discovered that his wallet was not where it was supposed to be. It could be...it *had to be* in his room. When there was so much time ahead to kill, the prospect of wasting even a fraction of it on a useless errand was extremely upsetting. This thought, once it took shape, plagued him even more than the possibility the wallet might be lost. Back in his room, he found a Malaysian cleaning woman with a dust mop in her hand, just about to work herself toward the night table next to his bed on which his wallet sat like a crown jewel on display. The woman, who spoke no single word of English, watched him with wide eyes as he took his wallet, counted the money, and slipped it into the back pocket of his pants.

"Excuse me," he said with a forced smile, as if to apologize for retrieving an article that had already slipped into her rightful possession. Following the same corridors as before on his way out was a disorienting experience because no time seemed to have passed, the light had not changed, and the false ferns looked exactly the same as before. The memory of the first moments after he had discovered the wallet was gone, seeping into other compartments of his brain, spreading out insecurity: *God, had he changed his underwear?* Because tonight would be one of those nights that would bring these private affairs into...let's say, sharp focus! *And...where had he put the tickets?* The idea he could arrive at the theater with Helga only to discover that he'd forgotten them produced a sudden knifing pain in his heart. *They were...* He quickly checked with his hand... Right! They were firmly stuck deep in the inside pocket of his jacket, unable to fall out unless he walked on his hands. *Yet…but was the date on them correct?* Again a panicky check. Thus, one disturbing thought bred the other at an accelerating rate. One of them reached his house back in the States: *could it be that the roof had leaked in the recent storm reported by the* Herald-Tribune*?* The thought of catastrophic failure came up again, of failure so complete that his life would be in shambles. He just knew he was a fake in his inner core and the time would come when he would be found out, as in one of his dreams from which he emerged soaked with sweat. It would eventually be discovered that his celebrated scientific papers were, in reality, gambles with the truth.

The wallet had cast a spell on this day.

When he rang the bell of Helga's cabin, an elderly woman dressed in an abundance of yellow answered the door. *Could it be…Helga's mother, whom he'd never met? There was some resemblance, yes! There was something about the curve of her lip, their lips.*

"I'm Adele van Wedelen. You must be Hubert. How do you do?"

"How do you do," he said, his eyebrows raised.

"Helga is on the phone. She asked me to open the door," Adele said with an inviting gesture of her hand. Despite her formal manners, he thought she had something of a squirrel to her: the swiftness of her movements and the curious look in her eyes.

"Van Wedelen?" he said, stepping in. "That's funny, I have a friend from college with that name. Victor his name."

"Victor! That's my husband's name!" Adele exclaimed. "Two people with the same name, what a coincidence!"

Helga stepped out of the kitchen and greeted Hubert with a quick glancing kiss, her greasy hands raised to keep them out of the way. She wore jeans and a turtleneck sweater over nothing. He was unprepared for the sculpture the tight fabric created, and he felt his body clock (*a misspelling, for once!*) start ticking. She had a Jackson Pollock apron draped over her jeans. How exquisitely funny!

"Hubert, you're just on time!" she said. "You met Mrs. Wedelen on the way in, I presume." Turning toward Adele, she said, "This is Hubert.

Hubert Belovski." And with a rolling movement of her eyes that said *isn't he cute?* she added, "We are going out tonight. To the the-a-torr." After a pause to let the piece of news sink in, she moved her head closer to Adele's ear and whispered, loud enough for Hubert to hear, "We're almost in business. The third one just called. And how do you like this: it's a man."

"I love it!" said her guest.

Looking for a place to sit, Hubert found the bedroom transformed beyond recognition. The big bed—the playing field from was-it-only-two-days-ago?—was folded into a brown couch. Next to it stood a small table. On the table were two of the tiniest china cups and an assortment of tea bags and spoons, all used. *What was this woman doing here? Van Wedelen?* He cleared his throat.

"Mrs. van Wedelen," he said. "Pardon me for asking. But has your Victor reddish hair? Did he go to Wellesley?"

"Extraordinary," she said. "Reddish hair—yes, it *was* reddish, though now it's almost gone! You know my husband, then!"

"Delighted to meet his wife." Hubert, nonplussed, got up from his chair theatrically and bowed in her direction. It felt as though he had rehearsed this scene many times. "He spoke about you in his letters," he continued. "Fondly. Victor…is he here in town with you? I can't believe it. I haven't seen him for ages!"

Victor…and this lady? He tried to pin down in what sense she fitted in his friend's life. The answer occurred to him as a one-word revelation: *fancy.* Victor had always had a tilt toward fanciness. That woman was perhaps a little old, but she was fancy, all right.

"Nowadays, I don't see much of him myself: he has some important business to attend to. But you must be *the* Hubert he talks about. He thinks you are special." She gave him a big smile, which amplified the wrinkles around her eyes.

"What is he doing nowadays? What's he gotten into?" Hubert asked. He was touched by the thought of having a separate life in the memory of his friend.

"He trades in building materials. Specializes in marble," she said.

The casual way she said it made it sound as though she was used to the task of excusing her husband's prosaic occupation.

"We are staying at the Hilton for a month or two," she continued. "I'm sure Victor will be quite excited to learn you are in town."

"Some more tea?" Helga asked her visitor, giving Hubert a quick smile of comradeship.

"No thanks, really. Thanks for the wonderful biscuits and the tea," Adele said. "I must go now. I expect him to be back at five o'clock today. We have a date: tonight it'll be the promenade."

After all the niceties were said and the visitor had left, Hubert moved next to Helga on the couch, placed his hand on her knee, and began: "God, I couldn't stand it, not being able to open my mouth. You see, it's all back, the excitement. I slept little last night. But tell me, how did you meet her? This is such a strange coincidence!"

"She just stopped by; answered my note about bridge."

"Bridge? Are you serious?" To him, bridge was old-fashioned, a somewhat geriatric sport. As a boy growing up in Germany, he had played skat. It was skat until dawn sometimes, playing for pennies and losing a month's allowance to his friends. Bridge was skat minus the excitement; it was like sitting around in a circle, knitting.

"Of course I am. Would I put a note on the bulletin board and then tell the people who call to get lost?"

A long, uncomfortable silence ensued. There was a fine line between straightforwardness and bluntness between lovers, and the line had suddenly been transgressed. The silence acknowledged that business as usual had stopped; what was left was an attempt to go back to the time before, when each touch had been preceded by a "May I touch you?" Hubert tried to guess the source of her irritation, without success. He decided that it was one of those things caused by the moon.

"It smells good here," he finally said with a renewed smile on his face. "Let me guess. It smells like...chicken."

"Bingo! Chicken, it is. OK with you?"

"Of course, I love it!" Hubert exclaimed in an exaggerated way, hugging her, sensing that her body was no longer stiff in his arms.

And then he mumbled, "Victor! Victor! Of all people! What brings this guy here? This town is turning into an attic of my youth."

"Gee, thanks for including me in your panopticon," Helga said, chuckling. "But tell me, how did he wind up with a woman so much older?"

"God, I have no idea!"

CHAPTER 11

The Circus Theatre was a gigantic building with a classicistic façade that formed one side of the Circus Plaza. To reach it, Hubert and Helga had to take the beach walk northward and then take a small lane that led off into the historic section of the town. The beach walk was crowded with people, mostly couples, who moved slowly, occasionally interrupting their stroll with a long glance across the water toward the orange ball of the sun. A soft breeze from the direction of the harbor carried a stale smell, the breath of a town that had not yet brushed its teeth for the night.

Helga refused to walk hand in hand, perhaps trying to avoid gestures she considered incommensurate with her formal attire. But there might have been a practical reason, too: she was dressed in a red chiffon outfit that left her shoulders bare and wore a white mohair scarf to keep them warm. The two ends of the scarf crossed in front of her chest, forming a "V," and she alternated her hands to hold the ends together. This gesture made her seem fragile, in odd contrast to the sight of her robust, cold-defying nudity just two days ago. Hubert, feeling hurt, fell into silence and displayed a well-meaning yet introspective face.

When he finally spoke, it was with a strained attempt to start the evening afresh: "The performance we are going to see is fabulous. You've never seen anything like this before."

"You really make me curious," Helga said curtly.

The evening had a chill cast on it, and Hubert found that as he walked, his feet touched the ground like springs, as though to reclaim a sense of initiative. *But the theater could... Of course! He should have thought of this before! It could be another test of his magic.*

Hubert had a way of making himself invisible at points of admission; his greatest feat had been to slip into a Rolling Stones concert at the entrance of Madison Square Gardens. He had developed this talent with some effort by turning a weakness into a strength. For years, he had watched himself falter in social encounters of all sorts; in the prototypical scene, trying to introduce himself to a group, he would stretch his hand out at the precise moment when the person his gesture was extended to turned away to greet someone else. With sinking heart, he would then address another person in the circle, only to discover that every word of his unfinished sentence had been ignored. He decided there was something in the way he moved, something in his face and voice that was singularly un-present, even subtractive. He finally learned to perfect the gestures and facial expressions that produced the illusion of his absence; he learned to stare five degrees off eye contact, past the left ear of his interlocutor, and to skillfully sprinkle his movements with bouts of awkwardness while turning his face bleak.

The mirror played an important role in his life because it was here where he was able to study the effects of his transformation, out of the world of noticeable physical appearances and back into it. He had come to understand that the exercise was not without risk; with apprehension, he considered the possibility that one day his rites of absence might reach a degree of perfection that would render his image in the mirror totally transparent.

When they approached the entrance, he walked two steps behind Helga and brought himself to think about farmer's cheese: the color of it, the sheer blandness of it, and how it was being made. A woman took Helga's ticket and smiled profoundly while Hubert weaseled by. "I told you so," he said to Helga as they merged with the crowd that was streaming into the foyer. "It really works." And triumphantly he waved his unused ticket in the air.

"Gee, I'm so proud of you, I can't stand it," Helga replied.

* * *

"That's got to be the plainest stage-setting I've ever seen in my life," Helga said as they took their seats in the tenth row, next to a woman who seemed to have taken a bath in concentrated eau de cologne.

The stage was enormous and surrounded by curtains. In the middle of it, toward the front, stood a chair that was slightly turned to the right.

"It's sort of minimal," Hubert said, pressing her hand. "The acting, too. It'll be lots of fun, though. Just wait."

As the house grew dark and the chatter subsided, a circle of light appeared on the back curtain. The curtain parted for a moment to let in a man in a blue uniform with a white sash. He was greeted by sighs of admiration and a round of fierce applause. He wore a gold-brimmed cap. His boots were heavy and black, but they were polished to such an extreme they were invisible except for tiny, brilliant specks of light.

"I don't get it," Helga whispered into Hubert's ear. "What's so great about him?"

"This is the Famashal. I'll tell you later. Just be patient," he whispered back, parting her hair with his lips and nuzzling her ear in an effort to keep her spirits up. "I read all about it. You'll see." She bent away from him, giggling, raising her hands in mock protest.

At the back of the stage, the Famashal was so far away Hubert found it difficult to make out the expression on the actor's face. But then the Famashal walked toward the front in ceremonial steps with his shiny boots, on a pace that was set by the raving applause, and soon he revealed a broad, triumphant grin. Hubert turned toward his companion with excitement but found her face unmoved.

Suspended from the actor's neck on a crimson cord was a shiny thing, a whole bundle of whistles, ordered by size and welded together in the manner of a pan flute. The house fell silent the moment he sat on the chair. With a deliberately slow motion, he took the trapezoidal thing—without looking; his hand was so sure!—and put it to his mouth to let out an elaborate fugue of piercing sounds, which critics called the *statement*, as Hubert explained to Helga. But before the statement was finished, the curtains parted at many places at once, and the stage came alive with girls, not yet sixteen years old, clad in flaming-red leotards. They started to move in the figures of a frantic dance, performing the traditional fire ballet, as the Famashal looked on, a touch of benevolence on his face as though reminding the spectators that it was he who lent glamour to it all.

71

* * *

"All right," Helga said, "now explain!"

They had arrived at a bar with an unpronounceable name that meant something like "Silver Trinket," a block away from the theater, where the play was expertly dissected by spectators dressed in black, turquoise, and blue. Some of the women looked like tulips swaying in a steady breeze. Some looked so perfect in their evening robes it was hard to believe that what they had to say could be anything but the truth. The words most frequently heard were "delicacy" and "frailness"; they conjured up the image of an actor who had kept himself floating three inches off the ground by some special kind of metaphysical buoyancy.

Hubert put his chin in his hand and shifted his head around in an effort to find an angle of best approach to Helga's question.

"It's sort of difficult to explain," he said. "It's something that originally started in the States. In the States, like where I live, many cities have local ordinances demanding that a fire marshal point out the routes of escape before the performance begins. It's like the stewardesses on the plane pointing to the doors."

"I hate that," Helga said.

"Hate what?"

"The spiel with the swim vests and the artificial smiles."

The waiter brought the Champagne. It was served in glasses that resembled a tall vase Hubert had at home.

"Anyway," Hubert said, "this guy comes on the stage in full uniform. Right from the cleaners."

"What's this got to do with the play?" Helga asked, lifting her glass.

"To the Northern Sun," Hubert said, lifting his glass toward hers and taking a sip. The glass was much lighter than his vase. "Well, somehow, the act by the Famashal—that's what they called him—got the upper hand. Nobody knows when that happened. But the fact is, people started to care less and less for the play that was billed and the cast whose performance the Famashal was supposed to protect. I think there is something special to the stage that is bound to lift a person with the right kind of sensibility into the world of...how should I say...appearances. All it took was a fire marshal who was receptive to the beckoning of that world. And you know what kinds of taxi drivers we run into nowadays: anthropologists, philosophers, art majors. Who knows what type of guys wound up in uniform on the stage back when it all got started."

"What was the real billing tonight?" Helga asked.

"What do you mean, 'real billing'? The real billing is the Famashal. What did the posters say? Famashal! The second performance is something of a ritual leftover, an obsolete reminder of an earlier stage of evolution."

"I get it: like the appendix. Like the intermaxillary bone. But what was it tonight? I didn't see a thing."

"Good question," Hubert said. You know, I don't even know. Some folk singer, I guess."

"How come we didn't see him? Or was it a her?"

"Everybody left. So did we. He might be playing still, right now, in front of an empty house. He or she, it doesn't really matter, given the circumstances." Hubert laughed and gave her a hearty smile, inviting her to join him.

Helga gave him a funny look and said, "You know, I don't really get these jokes. I haven't a clue what's going on. Theater used to have action, some kind of focus. This here is nothing but a ritual. It's dead. I'd expect to find this kind of thing in the Far East. Honestly, Hubert!"

"I'm fascinated by it," Hubert said. "Let me explain, all right?"

"Go ahead," she said, settling herself into a comfortable position.

She is really a sweet girl. She just listens when I ask her. That's something I forgot about her. Really sweet.

And thus he began: "Famashal, to my mind, expresses the essence of human determination. All that quacking and quibbling of characters on stage has been eliminated in favor of a pure form of theater. And you know, come to think of it, it makes a great deal of sense that a new form of theater had to spring from a non-theatrical tradition, so dead had your 'real' theater become. The act of announcing the location of fire exits has become a major cultural focal point, and you know why?"

"Why? Tell me!" Helga said.

"It's not because of the critics—they were, as usual, miles behind. No, it was the audience who turned to the truly authentic part of the performance, away from the stillborn soaps that mirrored their own boring existence. The critics had to follow suit in order to keep up their reputation of being in the vanguard."

"I'm sorry if I sound like a spoilsport, but this is conceptual bullshit. Go one step further, and you need no tickets at all. Or what about the pure performance of an empty living room confronting you on a Saturday night?"

"That's right," Hubert said, his voice raised so that some of the tulips and their companions turned in his direction. "Why do we need tickets at all to have a theatrical experience? And why do we need theater to probe the metaphysical depths of life? I tell you why: the reason is that theater-going itself is some sort of Famashal play."

One of the women, clad in a black dress that carried brilliant vertical stripes of orange, swayed in the direction of their table.

"If you don't mind," she said in a singing voice, taking a notepad out of her purse, "I'm with the *Daagblad.* May I join you for just a minute?" Without waiting for a response, she sat down at the table, briefly nodded in Helga's direction, and turned toward Hubert. "What do you think of the play?"

Hubert told her what he thought, expanding on the view he had expounded before. He was keenly aware of the possibility that he might be making history. A small part of a page, at least. A line, a footnote. Some critic would pick up his thought, give it ideological flesh, and incorporate it into something like the Anthology of the Postmodern Stage. Nobody would give him credit, of course.

Helga, watching the progress of the interview, emptied the rest of the Champagne into her glass. She took the bottle with both hands, as somebody might do who waters the flowers on the back porch of her house. She seemed to be determined to get drunk. The Champagne fell in a small torrent, and some of it splashed onto her blouse and made it cling to her brassiere. Hubert stopped in mid-sentence, watching one of her nipples emerge as a precise brown circle. *Circle Theatre. Private stage. The real thing!*

"Fuck," Helga whispered sharply, rising from her chair and storming off in search of the restroom. The tulip from the *Daagblad* gave Hubert a hearty smile.

"You mean this is all part of it?" she said.

"Yes," he said, "you could put it that way." He looked back at the journalist, suddenly confused. His mind was somewhere else. *Funny, what a small brown circle does. It's just a quotation. A quotation of nudity, and like any other quotation, it has the power to invoke the whole thing.*

The Lady of the *Daagblad* left, unable to draw another aphorism from his mind and apparently sensing that she could not match the sudden transformation of Helga: she wore a dark woolen suit, and her glass was quite empty.

"This cow has left for good?" Helga said, arriving back at the table. Her blouse was again immaculate.

"What did you do to get it dry so fast?" Hubert asked.

"That was easy. I stuck it under the blow-fan, the one for the hands," she said in a matter-of-fact way.

"Ingenious," Hubert said. The thought of her lifting one of her breasts toward this noisy contraption had a curious effect on him. He thought of several ways to make love to her without delay.

"You wasted so much time with her!" she said. "While I was in the restroom, I thought about this Famashal stuff and how it makes me feel you are on a different planet."

"And what was your conclusion?"

"That we are on different planets. Period. You know what I think sometimes? When you are really getting excited about one of your concepts? And you are trying to tell me about them?"

"Tell me what you think sometimes," Hubert said. He thought about the odd idea of dividing thoughts into those you sometimes think, those that occur with moderate frequency, and those that you always think. Was something you always think a thought at all? Or a mental state? He felt a tension in his body. He was clenching his fist. His knees kept moving under the table. *There was always something that interfered with the logical course of events.*

"That I'm not important. I think that I can be replaced by any pretty face. You are not interested in me as a person."

"What makes you say that?"

"It's just...what I feel. That's all."

Hubert decided that his fledgling relationship with Helga needed serious conceptual work. He paid and went for the coats.

"We'll have a nice walk. There's a full moon," he said.

"Oh, goodie!" Helga said in a mocking voice.

CHAPTER 12

The air was fresh; the promenade was filled with other theater- and concertgoers, who moved with a pace that was brisker than an afternoon stroll. Hubert and Helga talked and talked; sometimes one had to be immersed in the noise of a busy crowd to take strides and measure the vast space of the moment. The faces that rushed by, the quick glances, the silhouettes of hats and coats, the whiffs of perfume, sweat, deodorant, and brandy that were pregnant with cues; the promenade was a large, disordered dictionary-become-flesh.

They approached a brightly lit kiosk that seemed to hold an unusual attraction: a long line of people stood in front of the window where tickets were being sold. Stepping closer, Helga read the sign to Hubert, who was still squinting his eyes.

"Annual City Raffle to Benefit the Handicapped," she read.

"What's in it for us?" Hubert asked.

"All sorts of prizes. Here it is. It says 'A night for two on the Herengracht.'"

"Doing what?" Hubert asked.

"Herengracht is a canal in Amsterdam. There is this floating restaurant with dancing into the night. Spiffy place. I've been there. Not bad."

"California Sky. A top-of-the-line surfboard," Hubert said, now close enough to read himself. "Honestly, this is what I always wanted."

Hubert stood in line with Helga patiently, as if to earn some special consideration from fate for his civility. Both were giggling, holding hands, superstitious as all lovers. Hubert bought twenty-five tickets as insurance for a future with his girlfriend.

"Let's go to your place," Helga said as they strolled on.

"My place?" Hubert was dumbfounded by the suggestion. "You don't want to do this," he pleaded. "The room smells. The bed creaks. The single light bulb blinds. There is no shower in my room. I have to go across the hallway. How can you handle this? You don't even want to be seen in that hotel."

"I want to. I really do. It's only...fair. We were at my place last night. Besides," she whispered, "I've never done it in Aan Zee."

"Neither have I," Hubert said, laughing. He was puzzled by the fascination the hotel suddenly held for her. There might have been something in the way he'd talked to her about the building and its mysterious ways.

"But...," he started and finished, shaking his head and taking in a deep breath. His whole body seemed to rebel as he followed her wish and directed his steps toward the hotel. Only at the door did he realize that he should have been delighted, flattered by her curiosity: behind it could be not jest but a willingness to partake in all aspects of his life.

In the entrance hall of Aan Zee stood a group of four scientists, all dressed in trench coats, debating which bar to go to and waiting for more guests to join in. Seeing the couple enter, they moved aside to leave a path free to the stairway and fell silent. All their eyes were on Helga, and Hubert knew those eyes would follow her until she was upstairs and no longer in sight. He stared back at the phalanx without a smile, conscious of the silliness of his posture: a knight protecting his chosen lady from the lust and ill will of a hostile world.

"Ginger?" she said.

"What's that, honey?" Hubert said as he navigated her through this alley of eyes, past the poster with the matador, past an elderly woman receptionist who was asleep, slumped over her knitting gear. He moved soft-footedly, afraid to wake her up.

"There is this smell... I can't tell... I thought it could be ginger, maybe."

"If it's ginger—and I can't tell—but if it is, then I sure know where it's coming from: from the breakfast room; it's on our way."

Taking her hand, Hubert led the way. Her hands felt cold but dry and firm. They walked past the silent lights in the corridors, past all those numbered doors behind which dreams were about to be born—11, 12, 13.

"It's like being on some kind of treasure hunt," she whispered. "Much like crossing uncertain terrain before striking luck. But listen… something is odd: we never passed the twenties."

"There are no rooms in the twenties here," Hubert replied. "Don't ask me why."

"Why would they skip them, though?"

"The way I see it, this hotel is an architectural work in progress. It seems time has been introduced here as a structural dimension. Here, in one place, the roof is punctured for an extra skylight. And there, a wall is torn down. Another one is raised. The south entrance is boarded up. An entire wing is added. All rooms between 20 and 29 are made to disappear. Why? Why do trees grow? We are all part of a dynamic universe. Many permutations will be tried. Successes survive. I like the unpredictable element in all this. It makes me feel alive."

"Jesus," Helga said. "This sounds like we're back in the theater." She gave him a quick glance, apparently realizing belatedly that her remark was quite off base.

"You were the one who asked to come here," miffed Hubert said.

Helga pressed his hand and gave him a smile. It seemed she was trying hard to take the sound of her "Jesus" back. They went through a cloud of intense ginger smell, but this did not seem to emerge from the breakfast room; rather, from a suite of guest rooms at the south end, numbered 43a through 43h.

By the time they reached Number 60, Hubert's good spirits were back. He opened the door with a big, flamboyant gesture, as if to introduce her to the antechambers of a royal palace.

"Voila!" he said, giving the door a kick. It flung open with a neighing sound.

"You were wrong telling me how bad this place is," Helga said, laughing.

"How so?" he said.

"Because it's so much worse!"

He flicked the switch. The lamp did not work. In the dim light that fell in from the hallway, Hubert saw that a candle had been set up on the little table by the bed. Next to it was a box of matches, a generic brand. The local blackout was expected, and romantic remedies were in place already.

"I'll be damned," he exclaimed.

They both sat down on the bed, holding each other's shoulders. In this pose they watched the beam of the light tower the way honeymooners watch the Niagara Falls: as a spectacle specially created to enhance their own bliss.

CHAPTER 13

"When a cow is puking in Oklahoma, a cow is resting in Nebraska."
—*Jack Kerouac, from Trip Trap*

There is something quite unsettling about recounting to a friend the twenty years that have just passed. The wooing of a woman who is now your ex-wife appears as an inconceivable aberration of a person whose body you still inhabit yet whose feelings have become a total riddle. People who drove their cars the way he used to drive, with wheels coming to a screeching halt in front of the traffic lights—those kinds of people Hubert now considered stupid and asinine. Only five years before, he had picked up the habit of using his shirt pockets for coins, paper clips, and little notes. And now he was unable to remember the immeasurable stretch of time before, when those pockets collected nothing but lint.

* * *

Hubert met with Victor on the terrace of the Seaside Cafe, a converted ship whose mast and flags one could barely see from the hotel. It was permanently tethered with arm-thick ropes to two cast-iron pillars on the pier. As the ship rocked and rode the shallow waves, the strained ropes emitted sighing sounds as if they could feel the pull of the massive body.

Arriving late, Hubert saw his friend's heavyset body planted on a white chair. Half-leaning against the railing, Victor was watching three spoiled oranges bop up and down in the water.

"It's so good to see you!" Hubert exclaimed, shaking his friend's hand.

"Same here," Victor said, rising from his seat. "I ordered some apple pie for you. You always liked apple pie."

"That's right. My God, you remember things like that!"

The terrace was a place where seagulls dove from the sky, with the accuracy and suddenness of strafing bombers, to snatch pieces of food off the plates. Victor suggested they go inside after they had lost a good part of their pies, crouching over their dishes with protective, rounded shoulders.

"We must not forget," Victor said, "that apart from being a nuisance, these birds transmit all kinds of diseases."

Hubert recognized Victor's formal speech; in this unfortunate mode, when he was sober, he spoke as if he were quoting a turn-of-the-century encyclopedia.

Once inside, Hubert had the leisure to study his friend's face for the marks of time. It had grown more squarish, and part of its mass had spilled into a second chin. The eyebrows—what a disaster!—were entirely gone; the nose, once finely sculpted, was headed for a bulbous shape. The last twenty years had left little that was attractive in his friend. Would he ever talk to a stranger who had this kind of appearance? Hardly ever, except in circumstances demanding a humanitarian act.

"Yes, yes, who would have known!" Victor said over and over again, looking into Hubert's eyes as if he regarded the chance encounter with his old-time friend, brought about by his wife's passion for bridge, as the very summit of his life.

"Yes, yes," mumbled Hubert, not in his usual style and quite uncertain about how to make the leap into the past. He suddenly remembered an outing with his class in high school. Victor, who was one of his classmates, was bothered by discomfort around his neck. He then discovered the reason: a piece of cardboard underneath the collar of his new white shirt—it had never been removed. Victor belonged to a circle of kids who were so exclusive they would not talk to Hubert except when absolutely needed. Hubert watched him grab the strip and pull it out in several pieces, and he knew Victor had seen him watching. When their eyes met, Victor broke out into nervous laughter—the collar was too close to domesticity, spanking, underwear—and Hubert could not help but fall in with a hearty chuckle. From that moment on, things were easy; whenever he looked into his eyes, the cardboard strip was back again, and an embarrassed smile returned on the face of his classmate who was fast becoming his friend.

They had stuck together through some hard times in high school, and well into college, too. A woman then appeared in the album Hubert's mind was flipping through: Karen—an epoch of his life, and Victor's, too. There were pictures of picnics in threesome harmony, with her brown hair flowing in the breeze of a June day. Then the grave day when they both stood in front of him, hand in hand, with a story of their own about starting a life together. And then the two years of obsession and pain, intense longing, imagined love, of grinding in loneliness. This purgatory was followed by a magic day of light—as it seemed then to Hubert—the day when Karen "switched sides," causing Victor to reel and curse the day he was born. Hubert and Karen's ensuing days were fast and short, quickened by Hubert's sense that time had been irretrievably lost. His heart was a fresh wound, and no woman in the world could have dressed it without causing further pain. Those days were long gone now, pushed back by the accumulated random noise of living.

Thinking about a meeting with Victor when he had first found out he was in town, Hubert had imagined a hug, an embrace, and an unrestrained waterfall of intimate talk. Yet sitting barely three feet away from Victor in the floating restaurant, he was overwhelmed by the gray hair of his friend's beard, his bloodshot eyes, his serious asthmatic presence. Victor seemed to be similarly inhibited—although, judging from the glance into the morning mirror, Hubert considered himself much more of a whole—and with growing incredulity, Hubert composed in his head the story he would tell Helga: that after a bare twenty minutes of social talk they had sunk into silence, watching excursion boats go by, loaded with people who were either watching other boats or the Seaside Cafe. The sounds the cups of coffee made when they touched the saucers, the sounds of the forks after they cut through the cake too fast, the quibbles with the waiter who forgot the cream—those were the only sounds for the longest time.

Fortunately, he was able to revise his story. The reason for the change was that the Seaside Cafe closed at 6 p.m. sharp; the chairs were headed for their nocturnal place: upside down on the tables. Victor and Hubert rose, and the second they stepped from the slowly rocking plank of the cafe, Victor started telling him about his ex-wife, about the one before, and about the used-car import business he had seen all the way through a bankruptcy.

"Just when you think your life is in order, things fall apart," he said.

"I know what you mean," said Hubert. "It happened to me. Let's walk for a bit."

They followed the boardwalk along the cast-iron railing, toward the end of the formal promenade. A brisk wind came up, which alternately muffled Victor's voice and then exaggerated its sound.

They came upon a white mass of feathers on the ground, a bird whose wings were kinked in an unnatural way. Coming closer and curbing his pace, Hubert saw that the bird was sprinkled with blood.

"Look, a herring gull," he said. "Look at the color of its eyes!"

"Yes, such a funny kind of brown. Amazing." Victor said. "To me, though, they all look the same."

"Incapacitated. Immobilized. Grounded. Stalled," Hubert exclaimed. "You have any idea what that means for a bird? It's a fate worse than death!"

"A bee-bee gun or something? What could it have been?" Victor said, bending down over the dusty body.

"Some lunatic, I bet. I wish I could find the guy who takes birds out of the sky. No rhyme nor reason."

They walked further south along the shore, leaving the boardwalk behind, until the silhouettes of cranes and masts came into sight. Facing the harbor was a row of old timber-frame houses, and big painted signs gave the tired friends the choice between two bars, Beesters and Klabaasters.

"All right," Victor said, "we'll do Beesters first."

"OK," said Hubert, "and then Klabaasters."

They opened a massive door made of the planks of a ship and entered a world of biting smoke and red, steamy faces and grog. Brass lanterns and buoys lined the walls, and an entire mast with rigging was fastened to the ceiling. They ordered beer and carried the glasses to a small table behind a wall that was sheltered from the booming of the sailors' voices. An accordion played in the distance, but there was no telling in that acoustic environment whether the sound was live or came from a jukebox.

Searching through the rubble of memory, and studying the face of Victor behind his rimless glasses, Hubert found his way into another smoke-filled room, this one located in the Heidelberg of the mid-sixties.

"Remember the man with the diamond tooth?" he said, staring into the large mirror that duplicated the bar along with the bottles, buoys, and steamy faces it harbored.

"You mean Robert, the theater director?" Victor said, his eyes lighting up. "What was the name of the place? Starting with B. Balustrade? Bagatelle? Benefiz? Anyway, he had this black oily hair, always combed to the side."

"Yeah, strange, combed to the side, that's what it was," Hubert said. "And his wife—but were they actually married?—was an actress before she left him. Sometimes I wonder what became of him." Hubert looked into his beer.

"I remember the party after the premiere of this play, *The Island of Bunk*," Victor said. "Pretty awful play, actually. But at that party, it was the first time in my life I heard Jimi Hendrix."

"God, that's right! Can you believe it?" Hubert exclaimed. "There was just this flimsy record player sitting on a folding chair. I still see it in front of me. In the corner. That's right. I danced like crazy that night. It might've been with his wife. And it's Balustrade, it comes to me now. Balustrade, that's what it was."

"You asked what became of him," Victor said. "I can tell you this much: he runs an import store in Oberammergau. Lampshades from Indonesia. Hammocks from the Andes."

"Oh no, oh no!" Hubert burst out chuckling. "That can't be the end of a man with a diamond tooth."

"His hair is gone by now, too, I bet," Victor said, stroking his own with a satisfied grin.

* * *

Klabaasters was a vile bar that seemed to cater to sailors rejected by Beesters because of misbehavior and because they were stone-drunk. Hubert and Victor entered of their own free will, but they were not exactly sober either.

"Beesters, then Klabaasters, that was the deal," Hub reminded his friend.

The songs that were sung in Klabaasters were loud and obscene, and slimy brown specks of abandoned chewing tobacco littered the floor. The bartender dispensed the beer in front of a huge oil painting that showed a sailing boat on a stormy sea, and sometimes, when he bent down to get a towel or a fresh supply of beer mats, his head seemed to be that of a man gone overboard and in dire need of help.

It often happened to Hubert that noise of the highest intensity provided great comfort. Bending over to his friend, his lips almost touching Victor's ear, he now began shouting, and he shouted out a secret he never thought would come over his lips.

"A few years ago, I stopped reading the scientific literature. The only thing I continued to read was the stuff I wrote myself. When I tried to read the stuff other people had written—don't get me wrong, I tried very hard!—I had this feeling of unrest, of resentment.

"Victor," he exclaimed, clasping the arm of his companion with his two hands, "my scientific career is over! Finished! Finito! Aus! Kaputt"

Victor clapped his shoulder. "That kind of thing happens to everyone," he shouted back. "It's completely healthy to think for a while that your contribution is the only one that counts."

"But this has been going on for too long!"

There was a silence as Victor wiped his mouth and his nose. This case, the gesture seemed to say, requires more consideration. A clean start.

"All right," Victor said. "You know what I think you need? What you need is some kind of selfless act, something that gets you back into the habit of thinking and caring for people other than yourself. I promise it'll change your life."

"Oh boy, a selfless act," Hubert roared in a mocking voice. "A selfless act. Where would I start? Watch out for a blind person who wants to cross the road?"

"Where is your imagination? Your compassion? Just start somewhere. Let's see, who is the most neglected person in your life?"

"All right," Hubert said, staring into his glass, brooding. "My mother, I guess, but my mother is dead."

"Well," said Victor, "I'm sorry to hear that. But it's quite clear you can't help her now."

Hubert took his beer glass between his flat hands, rolled it slightly, and glanced through the brew at his friend.

"What's wrong now?" Victor asked.

Hubert tilted the glass this way and that way, deliberating. "A selfless act. Funny you should say that. Do you know this is the worst time for a thing like that? I ran into this girl. She's spending her vacation here. Victor, it has hit me again. I'm in love."

"You mean Helga? My wife met her. That's how you got ahold of me, remember?"

"This beer is getting to me," Hubert said. "Anyway, I'm crazy about her. The acts I'm headed for are quite selfish. My life is changing alright, but not at all in the way you suggest."

* * *

Hubert and his friend left Klabaasters quite drunk, and they might have been refused by Beesters in that state if they had attempted readmission. Yet even in the whirling state of his mind, Hubert remembered the importance of the next day's agenda at the congress. He bade his friend farewell, with a hug that brought him in contact with the stubble on Victor's second chin. Victor walked a few steps and then halted, turning around.

"Listen," he said, "have you been in touch with her since?"

"Who are you talking about? Karen? God, no!" Hubert exclaimed. "I was so glad to get out of that. Why? Why do you ask?"

"I was just thinking. At the time you took off with her, I thought you were such a son of a bitch. But now, from a distance, it all seems so funny."

Hubert started rocking his feet, his fists stuck deep into his coat pockets. It was getting cold.

"You know what she did to me?" he said. "You won't believe this, but once we were taking a hike through the woods and wound up talking about insects. I don't know how we got into this. But then I said something like, 'Insects, just like other animals…' and she wouldn't let me finish. 'Insects are no animals,' is what she said. 'Now, look,' I said, 'this is ridiculous. It's a basic fact. Every kid knows it. You can take my word for it.' And you know what she said? She said, 'Why should I? You've been wrong about other things.' There we were, standing in the middle of a pasture, surrounded by buzzing life and the smell of honeydew, which was created, by the way, to drive lovers insane. And what did we do? We were fighting about classification! And that was that for the day."

"Sure, I can believe that. Those were the kinds of stories," Victor said, shaking his head. He walked off with light, surprisingly springy steps, as if he were just about to start his day.

CHAPTER 14

*"If you find nothing now, you will simply end up with an apartment in
the City of Death"*
—Robert Bly, from The Kabir Book

For someone who believed in premonitions, there were plenty to
see. Hubert was awakened at six o'clock by room service: two
blue-uniformed boys who were scarcely sixteen entered the room
with smiles on their pimpled faces and served a breakfast he did not
remember having ordered. In fact, it contained items he despised and
would not have requested under the gravest circumstances: a grapefruit, served in a bowl of earthenware along with a jagged knife, and
a dish of milk-soaked Doctor Birchobenner's Muesli, a cereal that was
based on the many forms of the nut and always gave Hubert two days'
worth of gas and bad dreams.

At ten o'clock, the clerk handed him a letter as he was passing the
reception area on his way out for a brisk morning walk on the promenade. The envelope was white, embossed with the shape of a sun beaming its light on a nude couple standing hand in hand. It bore his name
in fine, curly handwriting. The ink was blue, as from a fountain pen.
Considering the fashionable disorder he had seen in Helga's cottage,
the possession and maintenance of a fountain pen seemed to stand out
as a miracle: somewhere in her domicile, he thought, there must be a
shrine of exemption where writing utensils and possibly contraptions of
birth control and beauty promotion were neatly stored together. Hubert
imagined a blue shoebox placed high on the shelf in the bathroom.

The sight of the envelope gave his heart a fast, needling sting: there
was no trace of a postal stamp—the letter had been hand-delivered. In
his mind, he saw Helga walking barefooted three miles straight; Helga
entering the foyer, glancing over the bullfight posters; Helga slamming

the letter onto the counter as if it were a legal brief, or something more final: a commandment, a bull, a white paper carrying the blasting merciless clarity of the Last Judgement. Helga, in the last picture, dancing and skipping out of the hotel like a little girl, relieved about not having run into the addressee. Hesitantly, he sniffed the air, sifting it for material traces of her, but it was pregnant with layers of perfume from all ends of the world; whatever of her fragrance had been there, it was lost.

He knew there were messages that could go either way; there was no telling. Carrying the unopened letter on his warm body, he thought, should make a difference. Thinking very firmly of a good outcome while clenching his fingers into a fist could change the text inside the envelope. Many things could go wrong at this step, so he decided not to open the letter until he reached the bathroom, the terminal station of his magic.

Opening the letter, he found that the text could not have been worse.

"Dear Hubert," the letter went, "I thought I could trust you. And I still believe I can. Yet your presence is monumental; it suffocates me. Yes, your love is a garden *(what conversation could she be alluding to?)*, but it is late Fall, and leaves must have a rest; their stems have come loose for good *(a phallic reference?)*.

"A long time ago, I really believed I loved you, but this time, I discovered my love goes no deeper than your skin. What's underneath frightens me: it is amorphous, formless *(once, he now recalled, she had called him 'fish, not flesh')*.

"Don't get me wrong. I wish you well *(the image of a train station, with him on the train: her standing on the platform, wearing calf-leather gloves, waving with a smile that hurts!)*. I have fond memories of you *(to use that word, fond, in an epitaph of a relationship!)*, and I wish to keep them alive, unblemished. By this, I mean without mixing them with future, unpleasant ones that are bound to spring up if we stay together."

To this, Hubert had several instant responses, but they were all mingled in his head and difficult to separate. *"She thinks of me like a goddamn piece of art,"* was one. *"Fond memories, that sounds like remembering the painting of a sunset by Caspar David Friedrich."*

"Escape artist," was another thought. *"She cops out as soon as a relationship is about to mature (come to think of it, that's just what she did the last time!). It blossomed, did it not? If she is so frightened of formlessness, why does she run away from so much beauty we created?"*

Then he thought about all the things he could have done, and still could do, to change her mind. And then he thought about the terrible finality of the separation — if, indeed, it could not be prevented by some deus ex machina, a messenger on a black horse blasting onto the stage with a silver trumpet in his hand, delivering a tune so sweet her heart would melt forever to fuse with his, Hubert's—about all the encounters that might have been ahead: trips to the ocean, journeys to Newfoundland, picnics on steep cliffs, hours of listening to the Bash-Bish Falls, those sweet-talking waterfalls in the Berkshires, and things as innocent and corny as making love under a Christmas tree.

That was the self-pity part. But underneath was the feeling of deep pain. As he read the letter, his feet carried him along the promenade, and the cries of the seagulls saluting their three embossed companions did not reach his ear. He found himself standing on the very spot where he had seen the little bird perform its crazy pirouettes, and for a short moment, it seemed that time had been standing still, because there was the same blue in the sky and in the sea that drank from it as he had seen on that day.

But now his face felt tired as never before; it felt as though it was about to come loose from his skull. He sat down and cradled his head in his hands. There was no bird this time to lure him away to some exciting adventure. The chance that had been given to him once was now exhausted; his wishes had been counted with the bureaucratic efficiency with which they were counted in fairy tales—one, two, three—and there was no appeal.

Deep inside of him, there was a captive scream and the sensation of drifting in a storm. He remembered a day in his childhood when the strong wind had played tunes on his open mouth as he'd turned sideways: this, he thought, was the only way souls that had lost their bodies were still allowed to speak.

Sheer fairness and symmetry seemed to demand a letter of reply, a similar declaration of spiritual independence. He drafted many letters in his mind; some were elaborate in concept, some baroque in style, but they always fell short of their goal. There was no letter that could express the pain and conceal it at the same time.

"Dear Helga," one of the letters said, "I forgive you, and I will never forgive you. It doesn't matter to me—how could it?—that you have decided to leave me, and I hate you for that. I have not been happy with you, and God, how I wish you were back in my arms!"

CHAPTER 15

"I gave her a Bedouin dress from the Northern Sahara," Hubert wrote in his letter to Eric. "A garment with the most beautiful embroidery. I'm not sure if you've seen one of those before. I bought it years ago on my trip to Tangier. On the dress, there were geometric ornaments in brilliant orange and carmine red. Attached somewhere on the seam, off to the left, was the tiny image of a scorpion stitched in fine silk. The scorpion was in the precise pose, curved like a question mark, when it inflicts the sting. The image of the beast in its deadly pose is the artificial blemish designed to spoil the beauty, lest—as Bedouins believe—the garment and the body it clads be consumed by the forces of evil.

"She wore it once for me when we went to a concert. I remember a moment during the break in the foyer. She came back from the ladies' lounge, descending the stairs, ten feet away from where I stood. The dress vibrated on her like a song. It concealed the form of her body, which I didn't mind because I knew the form by heart. To the ascending eye—I mean ascending from the scorpion in the lower left, skipping over two rows of circles and triangles in alternating colors of purple and carmine-red—her neck and head and her hair above emerged from the opening of the dress like a precious flower, like the fulfillment of a promise. "Do I look OK?" she'd later asked, apparently confused by the many eyes she had met during the intermission.

"Now she asks me if I want it back. The question hurts, that's what I told her. What makes you think I want it back? Yet what kills me is that she will wear it to please the eyes of a new lover. She might wear it right now as you read these lines. Perhaps she won't wear it again in public. No, she'll wear it on the couch in the living room at eleven o'clock at night, sipping a glass of Merlot, looking into his eyes.

"And the scorpion, by design, is close to her calves. It forms an iridescent spot in his peripheral vision; it will attract *his* eyes and then direct them to her legs. From there, his mind will move upwards, following logical lines, unstoppable. Come to think of it now, I should have asked her to give the scorpion back to me and keep the dress.

"I also gave her a little painting by a Bavarian naïve painter who came out big later on. A mountain goat on a meadow surrounded by wildflowers and *Latschenkiefern*, the floppy pines of the Alps. In the background, you see a pedantic version of the mountains. I'm sure it's worth a fortune by now. I wouldn't want it back either. But I'm wondering where she might have put it and what is going on in her head when she looks at it now.

"What do you think? Do you think I'm losing my mind? Instead of reaching out, my mind goes in circles: Where is she? What is she doing now? What is she thinking about? Is there a teeny weeny bit of thought left for me? Is she resting? Is she reading a book *(as if nothing had happened)?* Is she in the arms of her friend *(that euphemism makes it worse; that she fucks him is the real problem)?*

"I think I already know what you will tell me. You will tell me about women left and right, women in cars, women on the Autobahn, women in trains, women on tennis courts, women in swimming pools. Why do I need to kill myself thinking about the single one who is determined not ever to see me again?

"To this, I say, you are quite right, but it doesn't make any difference whatsoever."

CHAPTER 16

The seaweed formed unruly designs, like fragments of a dream. The first one was a princess without a crown and without legs. The one after that, just thirty feet away, was a flying saucer with some aliens on their way out. And now Hubert stood with admiration before the jagged outline of a motorcycle with three wheels. It was a certainty now: the ocean was dreaming of life beyond the reach of its water.

Hubert was on his way to the reception for speakers and chairpersons that was to take place in the pavilion in the middle of the park. Before the arrival of Helga's letter, this had been an evening to look forward to, one of glamor and evening robes. He had thought about strolling hand in hand along the promenade and through the park, a cautious chat about the future. Of this, nothing was left, and instead, he now considered the desperate new possibilities the party offered: invited female superbrains, by accident bestowed with youth and beauty, awaiting him with raised glasses of Champagne. Or a hearty welcome by Dr. Schivenhagen with an exclamation of delight: "Dr. Bolovski! What a pleasure! Your lecture was superb!"

Hubert considered the paradox that lay in the intensity of his feeling and, on the other hand, the scant notice the world took of it. The very waves of the ocean cried out for him; they clearly sang his blues, yet the morning joggers seemed to appreciate the spectacle as a mere fluke of nature.

He recalled the morning, weeks ago, that he had spent in the library, confronted with the evidence of his insignificance. The little he had accomplished had been diluted by the scientific babbling of his namesakes. And there still was the remote specter of an event of truly tragic proportions: any one of the other three H. Belovskis boarding a plane bound for Stockholm to claim the prize that was meant for him alone.

That feeling of insignificance was magnified now; it had spread out, from the confined cerebral space where his scientific ego dwelled to his heart and the body built around it in infinite layers. If Helga had asked him how he felt, he would have replied that he felt like a tiny grain of sand with a sadness so big it filled the whole world. But of course, this insight, like many before, immediately lost its weight because there was no Helga left to share it with.

A ship nearby blasted its horn, and in reply a large swarm of seagulls rose into the air. Their paths crisscrossed, each of the birds seeming to change its mind before going too long in a particular direction. *Seagulls were such chaotic birds; constant greediness interfered with a genuine talent for grace and cooperation.* He was convinced that if they only managed to act together, a flock of a few hundred birds could easily raid Aan Zee's food pantry. Nothing easier than that: Hubert had seen its doors open twice on a single day.

Suddenly he perceived the magnitude of the magnetic force the hotel exerted on his thoughts: it had become the single measure of his actions, his beliefs; he could start out thinking of his lost love and find himself in the hotel's greasy pantry. He felt irritated by this invasion of his thoughts; it was high time to leave.

Das Hotel, des Hotels, dem Hotel, das Hotel, he declined. *The hotel, of the hotel, to the hotel, the hotel. Aan Zee, Uum Zee, Iin Zee, Oon Zee. Ansatz, Umsatz, Einsatz, Aussatz. O, hotel, I hate your guts!*

* * *

The pavilion was overgrown with ivy. It overlooked a small lake. The sky was still too light for the stars to show except for a brilliant one that hovered in the east. As Hubert arrived at the lake, the windows of the pavilion, glowing with a mysterious sheen, seemed to beckon all Hansels and Gretels of the world to come in. Hubert looked for his invitation card. He searched his four pockets yet found nothing but small change. A uniformed man standing at the entrance gave him a warm smile before Hubert was able to activate his protective shield.

"May I help you?" the man said in a barking English, and there was no way out of this encounter but for Hubert to speak frankly about his lack of legitimization.

"I...don't...know how this could have happened," he stuttered. "Perhaps my jacket—I changed it twice today."

Incredibly, the guard let him pass with a clap on his shoulder. Hubert mused if this man had been instructed to listen for tones of remorse and clear signs of subjugation of the offender to the authority of the organizing committee. Hubert's meek performance clearly scored on both counts.

Inside, a flock of hostesses clad in orange blouses and blue miniskirts fluttered across the spacious rotunda in anticipation of the dignitaries and their guests. He was the first guest to arrive, and, fully aware of his pioneering role, he took a few steps onto the hardwood floor and bent his head back to take a full view of the crystal candelabra suspended from the ceiling of the cupola. The girls immediately took their positions at the buffet and the bar. Hubert, asking for a glass of white wine, found himself looking into the radiant blue eyes of a young brunette. She was surrounded by a cloud of sandalwood perfume.

"Where from are you?" she asked with a voice raspy from excitement as she bent down to get the first bottle from a case of bottles on the floor.

"From the States." Hubert looked down her blouse. He looked and peered and peeked, and what he did see was a white contraption that was the bare bones of a bra: a concave, lace-brimmed shelf, a scaffold upon which her breasts were resting, nipples and all; it was all sweetness, and sweetness so intense that it gave him chest pains. It was so much within his reach and, at the same time, so much out of it that tears were forced into his eyes.

"Do you want this Holland?" she continued her interrogation after standing up, once again concealing everything that had been possessed for a second by his eyes, and now her voice was that of a seductive siren, indelibly connected with the living, breathing things inside her garment.

"You mean, do I like it? I do." What else could he say? Could he burden her innocent mind with distinctions between the four countries he knew: Holland, the beloved land of Rembrandt and Kannitverstahn; Netherland, the boring, flat tulip land by the sea; Helgaland, or

Grachtenland, the temporary abode of a woman who had abandoned him for good; and Featherland, the charming land of geese, gulls, and mad, mad glass peckers?

Apparently, the two questions had exhausted the English repertoire of his long-legged interlocutor, because her face froze in an uncertain smile of admiration. It was now up to Hubert to continue with small talk, but at this moment, something curious and totally unexpected happened. A voice inside of him that he had never heard before started saying, *What's the use? What's the use?* As he heard the voice, his face felt tired, his body heavy. Even the glass in his hand pulled downwards with the strongest force, as if filled with lead. *What's the goddamn use?* He gave the girl a tired smile, turned around on his heel, and walked toward the piece of cool night sky that hung behind the open door. *Yes, there would be love again. Someday.*

CHAPTER 17

This land was one of the flattest Hubert had ever put his feet on. *"It's the flatness of this land that is getting to me,"* he wrote in his journal. *"Definitely, this land has charm. I like the people. But when I walk around, when I take the bus, I have no sense of getting anywhere. There is no sense of achievement, because the destination always looks like the place you started out from. There are the same telephone poles everywhere, sticking out from flat sidewalks, the same brick houses and dollhouse curtains. There are the same canals crisscrossing the flat land to separate the same tulip fields from the same pieces of pasture sprinkled with the same black cows. God, have I had it!*

The idea of visiting Aunt Frieda, which had started out as a project of humanity and goodwill, was becoming attractive in its own right, because it conjured images of mountains and valleys distinctly un-flat, images promising topological delights. Mountains implied the presence of hidden mysteries, things that were not handed to you on a (flat) silver platter but had to be sought out.

One of the tasks that separated him from the mountains of Tyrol and the smell of pine trees was checking out of the hotel. The task seemed immense, and he found himself twice standing in front of the mirror in his room, rehearsing the presentation in a firm voice. When he'd checked in, it had been for a limited time, yet something was telling him that he might be expected to stay on until he could prove that his financial resources were exhausted. At such time, without a penny left, his only option would be to take on one of those menial jobs of the hotel's staff: janitor, plumber-on-call, dishwasher. From the expressions on the faces of the personnel, he guessed they might have been guests once and were now slaving away to pay their bills and earn the extra money that would buy their tickets home. Of course, by that time, they would find their wives and husbands gone off with someone else, their houses in disarray, their friends moved somewhere else.

"I'm checking out," he said to the manager, sticking his head through the reception window with determination, anticipating resistance.

"I beg your pardon?" the manager said. *There it was.*

"I would like to check out." Hubert's upper lip was stiff with apprehension.

"So you don't like it here."

"No, that's not what I said. I'm checking out because I have made plans," Hubert said with a tone of defiance in his voice.

"What's wrong with your room, if I may ask?" the manager asked, leaning back in his chair and folding his arms in front of his chest.

"Nothing. The room is fine."

"So then, why do you want to leave?" he asked with a triumphant expression on his face as if he had caught his patron in a flagrant violation of a fundamental rule of logic.

"I told you, some important business has come up," Hubert said, suppressing an urge to grab his interrogator's neck with both hands and shake it.

"Couldn't you transact your business here? You know, we are well-equipped; we have suites, meeting rooms, interpreter services," his host said with the slippery voice of a salesman who has just managed to get inside of the house and has put the suitcase with the vacuum cleaner appliances down on the floor.

"What? You must be kidding. Interpreter services? Who is doing the interpreting?"

"Paul does. Paul knows Spanish and French."

"Who is Paul? The cook?"

"The very same."

Hubert paused, weighing his response to such absurdity. He then asked politely, "Who is doing the cooking while Paul is doing the translations?"

"I do. In fact, it was me who taught him how to cook."

"That's why..." Hubert quipped with instant regret.

"That's why what? What do you mean to say? You never tasted any meal I cooked, so stop insulting me!" The manager waved his finger in Hubert's direction.

"I didn't intend to," Hubert said, retracting his head from the window as if to escape the imminent fall of a guillotine. "All I want to do is leave. This conversation wasn't my idea."

"You didn't like it here from the outset. Your face! You should have seen your face when the coffee was being served this morning."

Hubert protested meekly: "My face was worn out from waiting for the coffee, not from tasting it." In fact, the coffee had been awful, a Croatian blend with an obvious addition of ground, roasted acorns, but Hubert had the sense it was not wise to bring up the subject of taste, which might confuse the issue.

"I tell you what," the manager said, falling back into his oily tone and working hard to bring a smile on his face. "You give me the phone numbers of your business partners, and I call them to set up the meeting here. Just some added service at no extra cost. We call it *personalized business arrangements.*"

"I will do nothing of the sort," Hubert said. "The bill. Can I please have my bill!"

"I bet one of them is Mr. Van Wedelen," the manager said with a smirk.

"What do you know about Mr. Van Wedelen? How do you know his name?"

The man grinned, shrugged, and said, "Just guessing."

"You know what the chances are of guessing a name like that?" Hubert shouted. "Less than one in a trillion! You must have been listening in on my phone call. Now I have another reason to get out of here."

"So, it *is* Mr. Van Wedelen! Just what I thought."

Intransigence, Hubert thought. *If I've ever seen it at work, I've seen it here. Shameless intransigence. Nerves. Mind-boggling rudeness! It couldn't happen in the States.*

"Now, look," he said. "I mean, really?" Stammering in this way, he made an attempt to appeal to an unwritten code of ethics of the trade and invoke the notion of hospitality as something sacrosanct, untouchable even when it is tainted by the touch of money. But he found the manager totally unreceptive to this appeal.

It took Hubert an entire hour to talk his way out and pay the bill, which was full of unexpected fees, surcharges, and small print. It took him another hour to pack and yet another to haul his suitcases back through the corridors, this time without help. That last conversation had left a bitter taste in his mouth, and he refused to take advantage of the last opportunity to look back at the hotel when his taxi took the final, obfuscating turn.

CHAPTER 18

The train moved through a flat landscape covered with the blue-gray mist of dawn in autumn. These were tulip fields, perhaps, but mercifully hidden from Hubert's view.

The idea of a train ride across half of Europe had appealed to him until he'd arrived at the station and been faced with the ugly details of the journey. There was the unwieldy baggage, a trunk filled with medium-heavy clothes uncommitted to the needs of the season. The weight was increased by the addition of gifts: wooden shoes for Aunt Frieda and six porcelain tiles depicting the six classic styles of the windmill. (Each of the tiles was wrapped in paper covered with tiny blue windmills that strongly hinted at the contents inside.) There was the demeaning struggle to get a seat in the *Speisewagen* at breakfast and lunch, because, inexplicably, hunger struck all passengers at the same times: 8:30 and noon. There were the ancient ceremonies of customs officers, who appeared each time Hubert had found a good position to sleep. Finally, there were the predictable fights with other passengers over the precise amount of fresh air allowed to enter the compartment.

What is left? What is left of the days in Scheveningen? New scars had been added to his already scarred heart; like the arm of an addict, his heart had no room left for new wounds. He thought about the bus ride in The Hague, when he'd missed the conference center stop, and remembered the joy, the exuberance he had felt that day, a joy that had embraced living and nonliving things alike: things that were simply ennobled by the fact that they shared this world with him and Helga. The flicker of trees, lights, and signposts rushing by had been heartbeats of hope.

That day now seemed remote; although there were scenes he remembered vividly, others were unreal, like inventions of a feverish mind. And yes, moving again, this time with much-accelerated speed, things looked different now. He now saw that the landscape did not miss a single chance to make him feel worse: NIVEA billboards at every station, featuring flaxen-haired, Germanic women much like *her*; sweethearts on the platforms, saying good-bye to each other with wet, promising kisses. Whatever he saw of human interaction carried a mark of certainty, of fulfillment. His only adventure ahead, in sharp contrast, would be Aunt Frieda, her animals, and—from her backyard—a view of the eternal Alps.

Somehow the scene he imagined was static; he had the vague notion of going on hikes in the mountains, but the task of figuring out routes, clothes, and provisions for these trips seemed to pose insurmountable problems, and so his picture of the time he'd spend in the new surroundings was rather that of an everlasting breakfast in the room next to the stable, with flies circling the pitcher of cow-warm milk on the table and Aunt Frieda saying, "*Ja, ja*," as she would dunk a piece of bread crust into her steaming mug.

A sound and a vibration penetrated the seats and the air as the brakes engaged, throwing the train into a furious staccato movement and then to a sudden stop. The old fellow who had to be on his fourth trip to the bathroom lost his balance and landed on Hubert's lap. Hubert saw the large pores on the back of the old man's neck and smelled an odor of mildewed cardboard. The man climbed off in a hurry, mumbling apologies. Hubert felt the urge to wash himself immediately, but he knew that the washroom, disheveled as it was by now, would only increase his discomfort.

Outside, a cornfield stretched to the horizon. The yellow surface undulated from a breeze as though nature had found a gentle way of continuing the rushing motion of the train that had just abruptly come to an end.

"Where the hell are we?" The voice of dissatisfaction was everywhere; someone out in the corridor even shouted, "*Bummelzug!*"—the deepest of all insults in the German language. It implied that this train had an innate tardiness, painting its engineers as outcasts in a country where punctuality and sense of duty were valued above all else.

Officials with stern faces rushed by in the aisle, shrugging off all questions. "*Unerhört*," was a word in the air: "Unheard of."

"Oh boy," exclaimed the old man, who had regained some of his composure.

"Oh boy what?" Hubert asked in a voice that did not betray his irritation.

"Looks like someone has pulled the emergency brake."

The emergency brake was the ultimate sanctum: its ubiquitous red handle in every compartment was an offer of control; a quick movement with one hand would stop five thousand tons of steel, make trusting passengers tumble inside, make them bump their heads against one another or against an AGFA poster of Rothenburg ob der Tauber, and throw three hundred business schedules into disarray. It would send an alarm to computers watching the orderly progression of trains that were assigned to the same track within minutes of one another. Hubert saw the spectacle with the eyes of his fellow passenger: the fact that the brake had been pulled in jest proved once more that Germans were unfit for democracy; that control could not be shared, and that it belonged in the strong hands of a few.

"Under Hitler," the old man promptly said, "this wouldn't have happened."

Hubert stood up in a sudden rage. He hated these old men who had learned nothing and still rambled on with their poison; he hated them with a passion. Under Hitler, an individual who was about to pull the brake without reason would have been spotted before he could even lift his hand; an individual like that had the kind of defiance printed on his forehead that could not go unpunished for long. Hubert opened the door of the compartment, now determined to proceed with his cleansing rites despite the grime he was sure to find in the sink and on the endless towel. But just before he stepped into the corridor, he turned and fumed into the face of the nostalgic man:

"Other things happened under Hitler, too. Other things much worse than your inconvenience. You know that very well."

The old man stared back at Hubert with an amused, inward-looking smile, as if in possession of a self-evident truth that had only temporarily fallen into disrepute.

As Hubert proceeded toward the restroom, his legs felt weak, as from an endless fatigue. *I'll be glad when this is over*, he thought. *Won't it ever end?* The train, starting as abruptly as it had stopped, flung him onto the toilet seat like a wrestler determined to finish off an opponent for good.

* * *

Even the healthiest of men become sweaty and tired from this kind of ordeal, Hubert thought when his nose acted up with a sneeze in Frankfurt. "Gesundheit," the old man said who was just leaving the compartment to get off the train. Hubert took his good wish for a curse.

A puffy-faced, heavyset elderly woman entered the compartment, carrying two boxes and a suitcase. She dropped her luggage on the seat and opened the window. Another big box was handed to her through the window by a young nervous man who might have been her son. When the train started again, Hubert asked her to shut the window. Then he got up from his seat to shut it himself.

"Leave it open, please!" the woman screamed, "I'm suffocating!"

Not knowing what to say, Hubert sat down again. Less than a minute went by, and then the draft lifted the curtain up and whipped it into his face. He smelled cigarette smoke so stale it could have been gathering in the fabric for several years.

"That does it," he said. "I'll leave it open just an inch."

As he pushed the window up, his sweater scratched his arms. His skin felt taut and sensitive.

"An inch?" the woman said. "That's just two and a half centimeters!"

"Yes, an inch," Hubert barked back at her. "An inch or nothing at all."

She shot an offended look in his direction, and he immediately regretted what he'd said.

"May I help you with those boxes?" he asked, noticing the luggage was still next to her on two seats.

"Don't you dare touch my boxes," she hissed back, placing her arm protectively over her belongings.

* * *

The skin of his arms and legs was positively hurting. He tried to shrink away from his clothes. He thought of retreating into his bones, shedding skin and flesh as useless stuffing. They would be mere buffers between his clothes and his true inner core. He considered the prospect of such a painless, etheric existence, but then he recognized its disturbing similarity to the state of death.

When Hubert looked up, he looked directly into the eyes of the woman. She stared at him with unabashed curiosity, as though she were seeing some of his thoughts parading across his forehead.

By the time the train reached Munich, his head felt hot, and the flicker of the light from the passing trees caused his eyes to hurt. This, he said to himself, is silly. Didn't I freeze my ass off on that cold day when I ran into Helga? And I sure didn't develop as much as a runny nose!

He decided to relax and appease his fatigued body with a hearty, slow-paced meal. The *Speisewagen* was five cars away, and the struggle through the aisles added to his mysterious exhaustion. Matters took a turn for the worse after he ordered a glass of Beaujolais with his meal; the wine went straight to his head and made him drowsy.

"Isn't this an exceptional day?" a woman said, sitting down opposite him. She was of undefined age, having a youthful face almost free of wrinkles but framed by gray hair. The way she was dressed suggested an age that was somewhere in between. She was Myrna, she said, from Innsbruck. She could be her own grandmother, Hubert thought as he introduced himself. He was conscious of a broad smile rushing over his face and of the efforts of his muscles to contain it.

"It is. It is," he said, hearing his own voice from a distance. "Though I need to keep the curtains closed because the sun hurts my eyes."

"Is something wrong?" Myrna asked and offered him some aspirin. As she opened her handbag, he noticed numerous little plastic bottles containing animal-shaped vitamin pills, non-aspirin aspirin tablets, and diet lozenges. They came in the shrill colors of Day-Glo: yellow, purple, and orange. She took out the aspirin bottle and offered it to him on her flat hand, reaching across the table in an Egyptian pose while her elbow rested on the menu card. He had a sudden vision of her as a traveling angel whose mission was to comfort travelers struck with the flu of the heart.

He was a victim of precipitous emotional drain. His body was an animal that was losing faith in the wits and determination of its soul. Of course, it would take a woman, a stranger, to restore wholeness to his scattered self. At each juncture of his life, he could count on the fact that there would always be a woman, a *dea ex machina*, who would collect his pieces and put them back into neat order. Here was a new goddess, and the machine that had produced her was the train. The fact that she had gray hair might have alarmed him at one time, but now it was positively consoling. All of her movements were graceful, well-re-hearsed. When she closed her handbag resolutely and turned her head to look out of the window, however, it seemed a gesture of rejection. He searched her face for clues.

He took the bottle between thumb and index finger and shook it. It rattled; there were enough pills in it to cure a horse. Listening to the sound of rattling, he had always believed, was part of the cure. He swallowed two, flushed them down with Beaujolais, and almost instantly broke out in a soothing sweat. He smiled at his benefactress, but his smile became a forced one as he discovered he had to hold his neck stiff to keep it from touching the sweat-soaked collar of his shirt.

"My husband just died," she said, still not looking at him.

"Oh, my God! I'm so sorry to hear that," Hubert said.

"He was a pig," she said with a voice that sounded as though she were scolding Hubert for bemoaning her deceased spouse.

"You should be relieved, then."

"I still loved him."

"I'm sorry again," Hubert concluded with a sigh, relieved that there was an end in sight to this difficult territory.

"You know—what was your name again?" she said in an animated way, turning her head back to him. "Hubert, that's right—you are kind of sweet. I don't know why I feel like telling you about what's going on in my life…"

As the train rushed through hop fields, green walls pierced by beams of light, Hubert listened to the warm tone of her voice. He had the sensation of lying on the hill back in his hometown, watching the clouds drift by. His favorite spot was surrounded by tall nettles and could be reached by following a secret path only he knew.

Hubert arose as another train passed in the opposite direction with the force of a hurricane. There was still the steady, calming flow of her words. It seemed she was approaching the present:

"...and I told him, 'This is it, this is it, I've had enough,' and just walked out, saying goodbye to his garden dwarfs, geranium pots, and dog-breeding certificates."

"I see what you mean," said Hubert, who had no recollection of her story. Both watched the telephone wires rise and fall outside until Hubert broke the silence:

"I'm getting a sense of what it might be like to getting old."

Myrna looked at him in surprise: "You don't look old at all."

"Really? There is something in my bones. There is a new heaviness. It makes me wish to spend a week in bed. But also, there is this sense of despair: for instance, I think about..." He stopped and looked at her, gauging her willingness to follow him. Then, perceiving a cue, he continued: "...about making love, furiously, incessantly, to friends, enemies, strangers, waitresses, stewardesses. There is this cosmic sense of irretrievable time; I feel it more now than ever before. I think that as we age, the intensity of this feeling grows, and the ability to act on it or convey it to anyone wanes. And being a scientist, I'm used to extrapolation, and I wonder what death might be like. Death could be the point, the precise moment, when passion about the uniqueness, the brilliance of life has grown beyond all bounds, just when the ability to experience it has shrunk to nothing."

Myrna looked into his eyes and nodded with a smile. It was one of those moments of complete immersion, as though her eyes and his were swimming together in the sea and the bodies attached and the train they were moving on and the landscape it was rushing through were completely inconsequential.

"Infinity and nothing," she said. "Death as a point of convergence. You are a scientist. I thought so. Go on, I'm listening."

Hubert didn't know what made him say these things. He thought perhaps her gray hair might have started him off thinking about age and uncontained passion. It was soothing and comforting to be listened to with so much care. Perhaps it was his own tiredness and stiffness that made him reveal those things to a woman stranger, because, in this state, he could not seriously be considered a threat. And so it happened that he received enough motherly attention and aspirin for his body to last well into Austria. Myrna was the first one to notice the white specks on his palms.

"If you were a cow, I'd say you're coming down with hoof and mouth disease."

"It's the first time I've been compared to a cow," he said with a laugh. She was pretty in a way and quite entertaining, and if he'd been less occupied with his own discomfort, he might have asked to join her when she finally left the train in Innsbruck.

At the stop after Innsbruck, he took a bus into the mountains where Aunt Frieda lived. Exhausted from heaving his unwieldy baggage from the train platform to the bus stop, he fell asleep. He was awakened by the bus driver: "*Das hier ist Heilsheim, hier wollten Sie doch aussteigen*—This here is Heilsheim, which is as far as you wanted to go," but his legs wouldn't move; they had turned into bulky, useless appendages.

He had to be carried off the bus by the driver and the conductor while a group of little schoolgirls dressed in blue uniforms looked on. Seeing somebody helpless had always filled him with pity and grief, but now that he himself was struck, he felt a great calm, perhaps coming from the steadiness of pain and the certainty that he would receive comfort from well-meaning people who saw him suffer.

Strong arms that smelled of tobacco carried him as far as the wooden bench next to the bus stop sign, where he was placed next to his luggage and where he attracted immediate attention. A minute passed, or two, enough for two villagers to step forth and try their school English on him, until two energetic arms parted the group of bystanders; they belonged to Aunt Frieda, a woman of small stature and wrinkled lips who was firmly expecting him.

"Hubert, *ach Du meine Güte!*—for Heaven's sake!" she cried out, grasping his hands and bending down to look into his face.

By the time they arrived at her little house on the outskirts of the village, he had been touched by many hands: on his back, shoulders, arms, legs, and feet. His head had been cradled and cupped on the way from the bench to the stretcher and from the stretcher to his linen bed inside Aunt Frieda's house. While his eyes were closed, he listened to many opinions spelling out the diagnosis and prognosis of his illness; words were whispered behind cupped hands. He knew that the ears of a sick man could be quite sharp unless they were themselves affected by the illness. He heard everything murmured, from syphilis to multiple sclerosis, and thought: This may be an interesting movie, all right, but it can't be a movie about me!

* * *

He was a granule, a coarse pebble in a stream of particles reaching from touching range to immeasurable distances. The particles had neither color nor texture; they were the very essence of matter. They were as much a part of himself as of the window he was gazing at. The stream looked smooth and silky from the distance, yet there was no light; there was no substance but the amorphous granules of the stream.

He thought he could distinguish a sound, such as pebbles make when they are being stirred underwater. He was standing in the slow-moving water of a big river with his head half-immersed, and as he moved one of his big toes lightly, a few pebbles changed their position, marking another state of the universe. And that "click, click, click" resounded in his head as if he had stirred his own brain with his toe.

And standing there, he became aware of his own breathing. He joined the air he breathed, turning outside in, like a snake that mistakes its own tail for prey and goes through doughnut shapes into oriented nothingness. Breathing in himself, his own body, was like an act of undoing the big bang. He breathed in dogs and birds, his mother and father—still in their featherbed—their forefathers and foremothers, farmhouses, trees and ravines, rocks and shells, sandbanks, waves, and more clouds than he could count. All that was in a swirling motion, entering his primordial nose funnel in a giant maelstrom. And after the motion had ceased, there was a single pebble left, surrounded by smooth, velvety darkness.

CHAPTER 19

Hubert felt the touch of a hand on his forehead. A little white-haired woman was sitting next to his bed. He noticed the octagonal shape of her glasses. The smell of sickbed pervaded the room, along with the soothing fragrance of chamomile. The white curtains moved and made giant patterns dance. Whatever world he was coming to, it harbored such things as moiré patterns. The laws of physics did apply, a thought that provided instant comfort.

"He just opened his eyes," said a soft, familiar voice in the Austrian sing-song variety of German: the voice that belonged to Aunt Frieda. There had to be someone else in the room, but whoever it was did not answer and was hidden from Hubert's view. But whoever it was, Hubert did not like him, and he decided to keep his conversation to a bare minimum. Then a phrase started repeating in his mind. *Time is of the essence*, he thought, unable to tell why these words would jump into his head.

"Tsk, tsk," Aunt Frieda said teasingly, now shaking her head in his direction, "isn't this the boy who caused us so much trouble?" And Hubert, who felt tired in every fiber of his body, sensed that a muscle or two in his face responded in a reflex of politeness to form a smile. *Time is of the essence*.

At last, a man with a white coat came into his view. His head was bald and glowing with a sheen of perfection as if he covered it every morning with a thin film of oil. His voice was equally smooth, and Hubert thought it quite fitting that he seemed in the habit of looking at a point outside the window when he spoke.

"What am I doing here?" Hubert said. "Who is this man?"

"Hubert, please meet Dr. Aichinger. He came all the way from Vienna to see you," his aunt said.

"But why?" Hubert tried to lift his head and sit up but was unable to move. His body had turned into a sack of potatoes, a giant piece of dough, nothing but a big hindrance to his will.

"Dr. Belovski! Glad to meet you," Dr. Aichinger said with a smile that looked rehearsed. His face was smooth, so smooth it looked as though covered with the thin polyethylene foil used for disposable gloves. "We have a little problem here. While you were asleep, I took a blood sample. It tested positive for coxsackievirus."

"What does that mean? I've never heard of it," Hubert said. "And who gave you permission?"

"It's nothing serious, normally" Dr. Smoothface said, ignoring the second question. "What happens is people get tired, run a fever, that sort of thing…"

"It's true, I was dreadfully tired," Hubert interjected. "I almost fell asleep with a piece of chicken in my mouth while I was having lunch. It happened on the train. That train seemed to take forever."

"…except for a tiny percentage of people who develop a complication. I'm afraid you must have been hit by this," Dr. Oilhead added.

"As a young boy, he always had problems," Aunt Frieda said. The reference to him in the third person sounded to Hubert as if he had already been abandoned.

"What are you talking about? How on earth would you know?" he managed to say.

"The pimples, the acne, remember! Your mother was desperate. She said something about it in her letters," Aunt Frieda said.

"Jesus, pimples!" Hubert moaned. "Aunt Frieda, this is hard. Something serious has happened to me; I can't move, and you talk about my pimples forty years ago!" He turned back toward Dr. Slimevoice, who had folded his arms in front of his chest, with the tubes of his stethoscope dangling down. "Could you be more explicit? Does it mean I won't be able to move? Does it mean I'm…paralyzed?" He felt a sudden chill as he heard himself pronounce the word. The words starting with "para" all invoked a state of imperfection; they were premonitions of doom. *Paralysis, paraplegic, parasite, paradox, paraphernalia, paramilitary, parade.* As he came to think of it, even paradise fitted into this devious pattern; it was yet another prediction of downfall, another beginning of the end.

"Your spine is affected. What we have here is a temporary paralysis from the waist down. The good news is that there is a chance of complete recovery somewhere down the line."

"Somewhere down the line? Weeks, months...?" Hubert asked in a low voice.

"Yes, weeks, months," Dr. Slimebug said.

"Can I get back to the States?"

"You shouldn't travel, period. Absolutely not. In this condition, you'd make it worse.

"Funny. Where I live, Coxsackie is the name of a prison," Hubert said, turning his head back to the wall. The wallpaper showed the fragile stems of the morning glory running up and down; the calyces of the flower were of a brilliant blue, as if so many holes had been drilled through the wall to reveal the cloudless sky behind it.

* * *

Aunt Frieda entered the room to serve him a cup of bouillon and a piece of toast. The specialist had taken the afternoon train back to Vienna, leaving a sizable bill and some instructions about what kind of wheelchair Hubert should get.

"Bouillon," she said, "is always good." In her smile was a hint of practical wisdom of the kind that comes from getting up every morning at five to milk the cows.

"Aunt Frieda, have you seen the package with the wooden shoes I brought you from Holland?" Hubert said.

"I did. They fit perfectly," she said. "How thoughtful of you! I tried them on this morning but didn't want to wear them. I was afraid the noise might wake you up."

The bouillon made him sleepy. His body felt as if he had climbed one of the morning glory vines right to the sky. Aunt Frieda tiptoed out of the room. The spoon slipped out of his hand, bounced off the leg of the table, and disappeared under his bed. He thought of all the things he had retrieved from underneath the many beds he had slept in. It had started with the chewing gum his sister used to hide. After that, there were playing cards and a color die. Then, as he grew older, the objects had become increasingly complex: there were kites and roller skates, a tape recorder he had found in a garbage can, and an old clarinet with leaky valves; there were the four linen handkerchiefs he used for masturbating when his time had come, and the shoebox stuffed with perfumed pink letters from a girl in Lausanne he had met once on a class excursion in the Alps.

Now it occurred to him, as the sheet of paper rustled and glided along the floor to its resting point underneath the bed, that this was the single comfort of his new condition: that he would never again have to crawl in the dust and scrape his back in search of elusive objects that had fallen, rolled, slid, tumbled out of reach, or of secret objects he had been forced to hide from siblings, parents, wives to avoid discovery of an incorrigible vice.

* * *

Hubert swam across the bay under the cloudless sky. The sun stood low, almost blinding his eyes. The hotel appeared to be beckoning from the shore, but something was terribly wrong with it: it was draped with a black garland that emerged from the entrance and ran in sagging semi-circles from one point of suspension to the next. "They have put nails in the wall," he said to himself. "They actually wouldn't shy away from that. They would pound fucking nails into the wall." A brass band marched importantly along the promenade, a sousaphone glittering in the sun. Then, responding to a command inaudible to him, the band made an abrupt turn to the right to face the calm sea. Marching on, looking into his eyes without blinking, but with a faint sign of recognition on their youthful faces, the players slowly disappeared into the glistening water. The brass instruments gurgled and farted, sending tickling vibrations through the water to greet him, the lonely swimmer.

* * *

When Hubert opened his eyes, he found the room half-filled with the light of the afternoon sun. A brass crucifix sparkled next to the door. His part of the room was cast in darkness. There was something terribly suffocating about this place. He tried to get up from his bed to relieve his bladder, and then he remembered his sorry condition. He called Aunt Frieda, but when he heard her slippers approach, he instantly regretted calling her in. It occurred to him that she was not used to added responsibility; in fact, he thought he had heard her sigh the last time he had requested her help.

"How are you, my dear?" she asked in a voice that immediately put him at ease.

"Fine," he said.

"You called me!? What's wrong?"

"Could you do me a favor?"

"If it's in my power. What is it?"

"Do you have a picture of your house?"

"Let me see. Oh, I have a Polaroid from when Uncle Robert was here." She went off to look for the picture. Hubert heard her go through drawers in the kitchen.

"Here it is," she said, returning with a beaming face and a photograph in her hand. "See my fat uncle in front? He just ate a schnitzel."

"I appreciate your getting this. But it won't do," Hubert said. "Sorry, this one won't do."

"That's what you wanted. A picture of the house."

"But my window, see? My window doesn't even show. I don't know how to put it. I feel like I'm inside a box, but I don't really know where I am."

"That's silly. Hubert, darling: that's silly. You hear what I'm saying?"

"The fact is, I don't know where I am," he said, "but I want to know it very badly. When I was carried in here, I didn't even see anything of the outside of the house. I couldn't see anything because I was in such a haze. I probably thought I'd wake up somewhere else soon, like back in my parents' house."

"When you are better, we'll get you outside," Aunt Frieda said in her most matter-of-fact voice. And she added with a smile, "and then you can look at our house all day."

Our house! Hubert fought against his embarrassment and managed to ask her for a bedpan, praying she would not use this opportunity to talk about his life as a toddler, as rendered in letters by his mother. But his worries were unfounded; she produced a bedpan with grace ("It's still around from when my father was terminally ill") and left the room when she was satisfied he could help himself.

CHAPTER 20

"Today is Föhn! Look at this marvelous air!" Aunt Frieda exclaimed, opening the window of the kitchen and leaning outside for a deep breath.

"Föhn? What is this thing called Föhn?" Hubert asked. "I've never heard of it." He was sitting by the pine table in his brand-new wheelchair. His hands felt rough from pushing the wheels, but he was excited about escaping the narrowness of his room.

"Ah, he's never heard about Föhn," Toni said, chuckling and turning toward Aunt Frieda, who had returned to her seat on the bench. "That's kind of difficult to believe."

Toni was a stocky, black-bearded man wearing lederhosen. His eyes smiled in Aunt Frieda's presence. Apparently, she also liked his company. He stopped by often in the afternoon when his carpentry work was done. Today he sat with Hubert and Aunt Frieda in the kitchen by the table, sipping a glass of schnapps.

"I can't believe we never talked about it," she said. "Well, as a matter of fact, this is Föhn today. This is unmistakably Föhn, if I've ever seen one. It creeps over the Alps, descends into the valley, blurs your eyes. It paints the sky an unreal blue…"

"An ethereal blue, a blue that makes your hair stand up," Toni added cheerfully. He was sitting near the window, looking outside, his arms raised as though he were holding a giant balloon. "Föhn drives people crazy; it makes the scalpel slip in the hands of a diligent surgeon."

As if rehearsed, the two friends fell into an elegy of human miseries:

"Cars drive off the roads, marriages fall apart…"

"It gives people constipation, blackheads, acne, asthma, all at once…"

"It causes nightmares, confusion, missed business appointments, partial amnesia, migraine…"

"Bad breath, accelerated onset of menopause, stillbirths, and bad cases of disorientation…"

Hubert listened to the litany with mounting impatience.

"But what is this *thing* that invades, drives, gives this and causes that? What on earth is this *thing?* How does it make people do what they do?"

"Nobody knows," Toni said. He had taken his seat on the couch again, and his hands had come down from their lofty positions.

"It's a great mystery," Aunt Frieda said.

"It would make you rich," Toni said.

"What would?" Hubert asked.

"If you'd find out."

Aunt Frieda nodded, indicating full agreement with her friend. Hubert, amused, considered the possibilities that might lie in a switch of career from fluid dynamics to something like Föhn climatics. Föhn, from what he gathered, went along with turbulence of the air, and he wouldn't be far off track in this regard. But as far as those strange effects it produced on the human body were concerned—those lapses, mal-functions, diseases, outbreaks, rashes, neurasthenic confusions, quar-rels of the digestive tract—he'd be hopelessly lost.

After Toni left, Hubert hurried back to his room, alternately whip-ping and braking the wheels of his wheelchair just as he remembered from watching Ironside in his pursuit of villains on TV. He didn't run into a single doorpost. Arriving at his desk, he wrote this into his journal:

Föhn: they didn't just make it up. It would be too fantastic; they are just too straight (good-hearted people, ruse-less, not ruthless!) to be able to con-spire like that. And the imagination it would take! Surgeons slipping with their knives because of the weather? No: I have to add this mysterious fluidum of the Old World to my vocabulary. Let's try it:

The whirlwind, the whirlwind, the turbulent twister that kisses the ground: Mother, the wind says, I'm here. He addresses the mother of all foul, bent, crooked, screwed-up winds, the thick fibrous, farty warm air descending from the Alps that gives birth to perpetual headache, Föhn without pause, forever. A wind with perpetual umlaut.

Isn't this the place where Heidi grew up? The following to be sung in three voices: Heidi's spritzy soprano (innocence literally bursting out of her voice cords), Grandfather's base, and Goat's alto vertigo:

The wheels of my chair/ where do they whirl? where do they wheel?/ The wheels of fortune, the whirls of forgiveness/ the wheels you don't see from the distance/ the whirls of tomorrow/ the wallaby, the whereabout, the whoozel, the wherewithal, the wereweasel.

In brief: where does the Föhn come from? It is the erratic collective fart of Italy, mellowed and aired out by cool snowfields and Enzian meadows and the soothing effects of high-power lines in South Tyrol.

In this country of Austria, there is no decent tornado, nothing that could lift you from a hopeless place and put you down with a gentle bump on top of the witch, at the beginning end of a hopeful road. Instead, the sweat and bad dreams and the pimples keep creeping through the cracks of the windows and doors: the Föhn, which makes surgeons hold their breath, which makes anesthetists step on life-supporting tubes and patients fall into despair. Possessed by the Föhn, drivers of cars gamble their lives away for an extra five kilometers per hour: there is an invisible, inaudible, untouchable, colorless fluidum that propels them beyond all sense and purpose; the promise of a vista not far away: is it a burning bush? A fata morgana? A field of clover with an extra leaf? A pie in the sky? A place in the sun? A final say? A handle on the matter? A night with Cleopatra? But they arrive at the promised site and find it much like all places before and all places thereafter: dull and uninspiring, listless, a place to avoid, a place to flee, a place to get the hell out of, a place that gives you the creeps, where the dinner is served stale, where the cockroaches thrive, where the showers are broken, where spray paint flourishes like lichen on gravestones.

CHAPTER 21

Hubert lay awake in his bed for hours, watching the light change from the color of lead to a bright orange and hearing every single rooster of the village greet the day. He thought of ways to accept his uncertain future. *I've seen quite a bit of the world. I can't complain.* He thought about the ingenious provision that had equipped humans with the means of traveling without physical locomotion: the mind. Having mapped every bit of the outside into some kind of inside panopticon, the mind had a stage on which plays could be performed in endless varieties. Here, miraculously contained in a small vessel, was the Grand Canyon and the marshlands of the Camarque, the majestic Alhambra, Freiburg's Cathedral, and Helga's breasts, all still in place, ready to reveal their secrets again and again.

A shy knock on the door interrupted his musings. Hubert asked his aunt to come in. Aunt Frieda walked up to his bed, a letter in her hand.

"From America. It just came with the morning mail. I thought it might be important."

The letter, which bore Eric's handwriting, had been forwarded from Hubert's most recent domicile, Aan Zee. It was covered with postal references: the franking stamp obliterating the pristine wig of George Washington; a hand pointing this way and another, larger one, pointing in the opposite direction; and a scribbled word, presumably in Dutch, along with three penciled question marks—Hubert recognized the confusion of the hotel's management with a smile. He opened the envelope and unfolded the pages with shaking hands.

"Dear Hubert," so Eric's letter went, "you always luck out! A romance in Holland with a girl you already know! I envy you. (Hope you get this letter before you take off for Tyrol)." There was a lot of talk about progress with his green sculptures, a whole page of it, which Hubert saved for a time when his spirits would be up. At the very end, Eric had added a postscript: "For God's sake, use your legs! You don't know what a gift it is to have legs that move."

Hubert let the letter slip out of his hands and stared at the wall.

"What is it?" he heard his aunt say in a voice that sounded concerned.

"Nothing," Hubert said, "I don't know what it is with this guy. I just wish he would write normal letters just once, like other people do." The phrase, "legs that move" stuck in his mind. At once, the consolation he had found in the idea of the richness of the inner panopticon was gone.

"I'm a fighter, I suppose," he said absentmindedly to Aunt Frieda, who was still standing by his bed. "I mean, when unexpected things have happened to me, I've always been able to cope. But there's never been anything like *this* before. I just have to get my act together."

She seemed bewildered, and eager to leave the room. Hubert sensed she was not used to being inundated with so much "talk of the world," as she was putting it. And surely, she was not used to having to care for a cripple—*yes, a cripple, what else was he now?*—in her house. But she bravely stayed to listen to his monologues; he knew that it was clear to her, after all, that she was the only one he could talk to in his present condition. For a moment, he experienced a warm, almost sonly feeling, but then all the worries returned.

"I'm a fighter—yes, but what can I do? I'm stuck. I've got to rent out my house. I've got to pay off the mortgage somehow. Where do I go from here? And my cat. Who is going to take care of my cat? What is going to happen with work? All right, I suppose I can take sick leave; that takes me to what? August? And then what is going to happen? What if I can't fly by then? This really freaks me out, you know."

"What does that mean: 'freaks me out'?" his aunt asked.

"Upsets me. Disturbs me. Whatever."

"One step at a time," she said. "However long you have to stay here, I'll take good care of you."

"You are so kind to me," he said. "Without you, I'd still be lying on that bench by the bus stop."

"Hubert, you are so funny sometimes!" Aunt Frieda said, shaking with laughter. "Still lying on that bench!"

"I was thinking, the thing to worry about is my lab," Hubert continued. "The other thing to worry about is the house. Which one first? And what will happen to Sunshine? That poor creature probably won't recognize me anymore."

"Sunshine? Who is Sunshine?"

"My orange-colored, fluffy-furred, mixed-breed, greedy-sneaky cat."

"Oh," Aunt Frieda said.

Sunshine! What he would give to have him here. Those had been happy times when he'd chased the cat through the entire house, swearing. By using a sixth sense, the animal could always tell whether his master's intentions were friendly, or whether he was thinking about clipping his nails. And when Sunshine was finally cornered next to the radiator in the dining room, the cat would stare at him with alienation and intense fear, as though expecting to be instantly executed by a friend that had gone insane.

"First things first," he continued, taking mental notes. "The cat. Need to send telegram to Eric regarding Sunshine."

"Who is this Eric again?"Aunt Frieda asked.

"Eric. My friend Eric, you know? The one who just wrote me the letter. Actually, he wrote it quite a while ago, but it took some time to get here. Anyway, he's the one who got Sunshine now. He lives with his sister. I'll let him keep the cat for a while. He can do something for me, after all. That's OK. That part is going to be easy. Now item Number Two: the house. Two bedrooms, should sleep two student couples. Easily. *(Funny expression in English: a room sleeping people!)* Could work out. Who looks after the house, though? In my neighborhood, you know what happened once: there was this well-kept house, spiffy, with curtains and all that. Then these people got divorced, rented it out to students. Within a year, trash everywhere. The swimming pool collapsed. Windows broken. A miserable sight. I don't know why they didn't sell it before it got so run down. Perhaps they didn't want to make things final."

"The doctor says you can probably transfer back to the States in a month or two, once your condition has stabilized," Aunt Frieda said.

"Transfer? I love that expression. Makes me feel alive like a piece of furniture. Anyway, where was I? I need somebody to look after the house. Someone from my lab? Rich Fletcher the technician, perhaps. Decent guy. Come to think of it, he is the right man to ask. Write letter to him. Next, the lab. Write to boss. Formalize leave of absence. Cut in pay? Quite likely. What percentage? Could Heilsheim be acceptable as a place for sabbatical stay? Haha! Fantastic research possibilities! Turbulence phenomena associated with temperature inversion during Föhn. To be published in *Torque and Curl.* Or in *Weather Phenomena Monthly*. Or in *Whirl View.* How does that sound, Aunt Frieda?"

"You sound like a real professor," she said. "I didn't come across that many, but that's what you sound like."

"Check village library for books on thermodynamics. Interlibrary loan? Inexpensive xeroxing? Professional personnel?" he said, immersed in his thoughts.

"Minnie is the one who runs the library," Aunt Frieda said. "Essentially by herself. She has this one son who is retarded. She lives… I feel silly. I forgot the name of the street. They live…"

"It's not so important now," Hubert said.

"But I don't know about those thermos things in the library. You'll find all kinds of other things. And they have a big section on children's books." She looked at the clock. "Maria and Joseph!" she cried out. "The goat will be starving. That poor thing."

"The goat? You have a goat?"

"Remember what you drank this morning? That was goat's milk."

"I drank goat's milk? Yuk." Hubert cringed and contorted his face. His aunt laughed heartily as she got up from her chair.

"You better watch out!" she crowed in a voice like the Witch of the West, bending her shoulders and waving a finger at him in mock admonishment. "I have all kinds of secret animals. You'll taste the milk of creatures you've never heard of."

This was the second time he had seen her laugh. *The sorts of things we've got in this house!* he said to himself. *I've got a broken spine. She's got a sense of humor. I got to drink goat's milk every morning. Lucky me. Things can only get better.*

After Aunt Frieda left, Hubert picked up Eric's letter again. He tried to read the page he'd skipped before, but it was not easy. In the letter, his friend talked about things that now seemed centuries away:

We've built a glasshouse and keep it at 85 degrees. You should see these plants; they are unbelievable. From the way they grow, we'll have three seasons at least. All molds are in place, some gourds are already done, and new female flowers are still sprouting! And we are keeping some bees to do the pollination. Stewart brought his girlfriend here, and later she brought the others from Macy's, where she works. It was an absolute riot. You should have seen the crowd. Some of the molds are filled to the brim, like bras in a Miss America competition (this actually gave me a new idea!). We took the molds off and left those green bastards on the vine to show them off. They look unreal. Green heads, hanging upside down, sort of looking at each other. Leaving them on for a while actually makes them more interesting; once out of confinement, they develop irregularities. A bump on the nose, an oblique extension of the skin, a mole on the forehead. Break of symmetries, I think that's how you would put it. Stupendous. What I wanted to ask you: is there any chance, if I go on with this for a few generations, and use the same mold over and over again so that the plant—how should I put it?—gets used to it, is there any chance they'd grow like this on their own? Wasn't that what good old Darwin said? It would save me a lot of money; all this screwing around with molds and what have you. And then I could even think of selling the seeds.

CHAPTER 22

"*MONDAIN VERMAAK OP SCHEVENINGEN BOULEVARD,*" Hubert typed in capital letters—"*FASHIONABLE AMUSEMENT ON THE SCHEVENINGEN BOULEVARD.*" Aunt Frieda had bought him a used portable typewriter for his birthday. The typewriter, a bottle of the finest Enzian schnapps, and five hundred sheets of good white stock with the Monk watermark, neatly stacked on the table against the wall, still within his reach.

While the wheelchair freed his body, at least to some extent, the typewriter gave wings to his mind. Since it had arrived two months before, Hubert had been a changed man. Gone were the hours of brooding; instead, he started to fill pages with something he called *quickthoughts*: things that came to his mind without reflection. True to his vocation in science, the resulting statements had a random, swirly quality, as if words had been lifted up and scattered by a storm. He had started numbering them and added little symbols—"H" for Helga, "E" for Eric, "G" for general, and "@" for matters worth coming back to. And there was "TBLU," for things better left untouched.

He studied the postcard of the Scheveningen Boulevard he had bought the evening before he'd left Holland. It showed the stretch of the promenade where he and Helga had slowed down, where they had listened to the soft, periodic rush of the waves and spoken to each other for the last time with total openness. The picture gave but a small glimpse of the universe, yet he was awed by its richness. It contained pointers to mysterious worlds, but also mundane things such as trees that required no explanation. And sprinkled in between were capricious nonsensical details: they seemed to be placed there by *someone* or *something* to mock the ordering mind. The picture was spacious: taken with a wide-angle lens from a vantage point high above street level, perhaps from one of the grand hotels' fifth-floor balconies. As his eyes wandered from the cafe tables in the foreground to the silhouettes of the cranes in the back, he thought about buzzing across that expanse in his wheelchair with enormous speed, ringing the bell to clear the way whenever the clusters of evening strollers became impenetrable.

Hubert stared at the photograph, hoping to find a sign that would help him understand the forces that had catapulted him from the promenade to the place behind the typewriter in Aunt Frieda's guest room, a good thousand kilometers away. He looked at the scene for a point of entry and departure. The longer he stared, the more he became convinced that a most meticulous list was needed: a list of references to the world to the east and west of the frame, beyond the horizon and behind the invisible eye of the camera. An exhaustive list of all things in this microcosm, touched as they were by human folly and ingenuity, could enable him to grasp the world outside of it. Like a spider, able to move swiftly from the inner court of its web along strong threads to the points of support, he might be able to travel along threads that linked the scene in the picture to the firm space surrounding it. In this thought he recognized his desire to be able to transcend the bounds of his present condition, to dismiss them as trivial obstacles to his quest for knowledge and love.

Thus, underneath the curious title of the postcard, Mondain Vermaak, he started his list:

> *1. 1 crane (in the distance; hardly noticeable): The crane, the sign of the cross magnified to (G) Godzilla scale—but this is all dunked in darkness at this hour. The harbor smells silently, without a single light.*
>
> *2. 13 gaslight-style candelabras: Let us not quibble about the true number; the smallest change of perspective might have included the fourteenth. I even know where I'd put it, but this has no significance. But the balls, I find them hard to bear: four glowing balls pointing into the sky, as if Super Bull were rolling on his back like a dog playing dead.*
>
> *3. 1 black dog (moved during exposure): There he is, and naturally keen to escape the scene.*
>
> *4. 15 empty chairs (changes rapidly; average occupancy is 35*

minutes). Calm anticipation in a piece of furniture that has every reason to go insane. Catalogue says: steel chair, suspends gravity, lets rainwater pass—a jewel, in one word. But no word from Susan, the packer, such as in "hand-packed and tested by Susan." Send this label in if not entirely (!) satisfied. (H) Susan's little ass might have started them all; hence, their perpetual melancholy.

5. 3 empty tables with red tablecloths: (TBLU) Well, well; tables escape such ordeals; they cater to higher body functions and have a flatness about them that makes it difficult to develop visceral feelings. What counts in the end is their lack of crookedness, the ability of their four legs to behave like three on a non-Euclidean plane, especially if elbows are resting on both sides.

6. 1 empty ashtray: Slurped empty by a penniless nicotine addict who has just been refused a cigarette by three elderly men sitting on some of the occupied chairs (see below). Anyway, it is sparkling clean now: part of the invitation.

7. 655 occupied chairs: The things that people do to stay away from home! (E) The prices they pay! The kind of service they tolerate! But I cannot blame them: there is the night air, the sounds of the waves, and the idea that except for trifles like the overflowing garbage can and the poor drunk who is drunk because he is poor and poor because he is drunk, except for trifles like this—and on a night like this I could not think of many more—the world is basically a sound place.

8. 2 bus shelters (occupied): There are no buses at this hour on Scheveninger Boulevard. Everybody knows this except for the tourists who have been sitting here for a good hour. Much of the conversations in the cafe circle around the lot of these people: where they might want to go and when they will find out about their predicament.

9. 6 garbage cans (one overflowing): These are pre-sorting devices designed to eliminate organic refuse within five minutes and without trace. Essentially five thousand seagulls are in the employ of the city, and amongst themselves, they have worked out a system of dispatching that is free from bureaucratic intervention. (Note: the overflowing can is filled with indigestible copies of the DAAGBLAD, the daily paper.)

10. 5 benches overlooking the beach (an undetermined number hidden by bus shelters): This is the time for lovers to look into the direction of the sunset they have missed because of heavy petting in the car. Sweet soreness in (H) their private parts.

11. 1 apparent drunk (Notice lack of balance! Dishevelled look!): If I'm right, he throws up because the ashes are filled (TBLU) with heavy metal salts and traces of dioxin.

Hubert's room was neatly organized; on Aunt Frieda's request, Toni had installed a bench that ran along the entire length of the back wall of the room, and on it, Hubert had arranged his typewriter, his Webster, the Duden, its authoritative German equivalent, along with French and Dutch dictionaries and a pile of books on turbulence he'd ordered from the nearest serious library, the Innsbruck's *Hofbibliothek*. There was the pile of his unfinished manuscripts and a Krups coffee-making machine that was now purring and steaming to produce the second brew of the day.

The weather outside was miserable; the rain hit the glass of the window in gushes. Aunt Frieda had mentioned something about a school-teacher wanting to stop by to meet him. Hubert anticipated the visit with mixed feelings. He was alone, in bad need of someone to talk to about things beyond Föhn and the well-being of the goat. But he also thought of village teachers as encrusted ideologues of the status quo, and silently braced himself for a battle. He rolled his wheelchair to the window. From there, he looked at the trees bending in the storm and the curtains of water in the air that all but concealed the mountaintop, and sighed. For once, it felt good to be in the house. Back at the typewriter, he went on with his oeuvre:

12. 7 seagulls (give or take one): These form the vanguard of the city's sanitary crew: wings like steel and eyes sharp as needles.

13. 2000 tiles (light brown): A conservative estimate.

14. The spaces between the tiles, filled with mortar: We come to fillers now. The evening comes to a close. Apologies are mumbled. Bills are added up.

15. 600 tiles (black): Same story. I hope there'll be no quarrel now, even though the bills are clearly inflated.

16. The spaces between the black tiles, filled with mortar: Chairs are being pushed back, into an uncertain waiting mode.

17. The expression of unabashed tourist interest on a blonde (H) woman's face (nearest table on the left; I've never seen this woman).

There was a knock on the door, and a tall, skinny man entered, let in by Aunt Frieda. His loden jacket was soaked with water, leaving little puddles on the floor. He had a black mustache and the sharp eyes of a buzzard. Within a few seconds, he had taken inventory of all items in the room.

"Hubert, this is Herr Krantz, the schoolteacher," Aunt Frieda said.

"Guten Tag. It's a pleasure to meet you," Hubert said, extending his hand for a handshake.

"Guten Tag, Herr Doctor Belovski. The pleasure is all mine," Krantz said. His hand felt wiry and surprisingly warm.

"You are all wet!" Hubert exclaimed. "I'm sure my aunt has a good place for your coat. Take a seat!"

Without a word, apparently miffed by the indirect order, Aunt Frieda took Krantz's dripping coat and disappeared into the hallway.

"Thanks," Krantz said and sat down on the wooden chair next to Hubert's bed. "My students have told me a lot about you." It was quite possible that he told the truth; two boys from his second-grade class were in the habit of stopping by at Frieda's house on their way home; they always got a treat: a cup of hot chocolate, a cherry-flavored candy or a chat about this mysterious place called America. Incredulous, they had learned that there was snow in America, a land they'd imagined as a desert full of horses and cowboys, with skyscrapers neatly placed around the edges. Stepping closer, the teacher's eyes fell on the page Hubert was working on.

"Busy so early?"

"It's my form of recreation," Hubert said. "And I get up with Aunt Frieda's chickens."

"That's right; they don't know about Saturdays," Krantz said. "May I ask what you're working on?"

"I call them quickthoughts, or enumerations. I believe the future of literature lies in enumeration."

"Enumeration. Enumeration?"

"Basically, lists of things and thoughts they invoke. Following our primary experience, unedited. Listening to our unconscious, if you will."

"That's probably as far as you can get away from Ganghofer," Krantz said. "And what will happen to the fabric of fiction? Think of the kind of math you'd get if all you did was count," he continued, raising his voice as if he wanted to fend off objections to his objections in advance. And then he added in a different, confiding voice, "You know, I had this boy in my class; once, after school, he asked to talk to me, and do you know what he said? He said, 'Herr Krantz, I hate it. I really hate knowing that numbers don't stop. It gives me the creeps.' So, I had to spend an hour with him, calming him down, telling him that everything else had an end to it. That numbers didn't matter because they were all made up anyway."

"Quite a story!" Hubert said.

"You don't know what schools are like up here. I'm not just the math teacher; I'm just about everything. Between me and the priest, we better have the answers."

Krantz got up from his chair and walked to the window. He lifted the curtain and wiped the glass, which had been blanketed by condensing water. He took a look outside.

"You must be spending a lot of time trying to be serious," Hubert said.

"Correct," the teacher said, turning around, tight-lipped. "I think the clouds are opening up. The sun may be back later this afternoon."

"What happened to the boy?" Hubert asked.

"What boy?" Krantz asked.

"The one with the infinity problem."

"I'll have to watch him. Seriously. Depression can start that way. I'm giving him things to do during math."

"Like what?"

"Things to calm him down. Like coloring the flowers of the Alps in our coloring book. Such as *Enzian, Samtpfötchen*, and *Edelweiss*. It gives him confidence in something he knows."

There was a long, uncomfortable pause because the definite end of this subject had been reached. Hubert found himself wanting to ask more personal questions, but something kept him from doing this. Krantz left soon afterward, explaining that he needed to go on an errand. After the door closed behind him, Hubert mumbled, "I should have thought of something to offer him. A schnapps, or something." He felt a pang of disappointment but was at a loss to explain why. Perhaps he recognized some likeness: could it be that this wiry man was just as stranded as he?

Hubert saw the beginning of a social network in the tiny village. Aunt Frieda and her regular *beau*, Anton, curious Krantz, himself, the priest, and perhaps even the crazy baker his aunt had mentioned. Eventually, there could be others, too, by the time he got around. He contemplated the curious trade-off between mobility and depth of interaction. When he was still in command of his legs, he had used them mostly to escape: away from each person before there even was a chance that a chord of friendship could be struck. Now that he was virtually glued to the same spot, he found himself anticipating the next visit of a man he might have easily overlooked before.

Instead of continuing with his list, he put a new page into his typewriter and started the long-overdue reply to his friend:

Dear Eric:

Thanks for your letter. I meant to write to you earlier, but I was kind of stuck. Ever hear of Lamarck? He was this 18th-century twerp who believed in the inheritance of acquired traits. Well, he was plainly wrong. The genes just don't work that way. But just to check it yourself, you could leave the muzzle off a few of your green friends. One of those faces might just pop up by chance. Think of ginseng roots: bifurcated, they are, like legs, often with private parts attached. I found a tomato once with a little penis stuck to it.

A red little fellow, even with tiny balls. (Pears, incidentally, always have a sad expression even though they don't have much of a face.)

More some other time. Right now, I'm too busy doing things outside. I climbed a few mountains already. Those eternal Alps! They are fantastic!

Hubert.

P.S.: Are you really sure you want to go ahead with this garden stuff in a big way?

* * *

Hubert waited a few measured days and then called Krantz to invite him for some schnapps.

"Wie geht's, Dr. Belovski? Still making lists?" Krantz said as he cheered his host with his first glass of *Enzian*.

"OK. The lists were getting out of hand. I slowed down a bit."

"Everything else fine?" Krantz pointed in the direction of the kitchen.

"Ah, my aunt? She is a soul of a person," Hubert replied.

"I feel a bit silly," he added after a brief pause. "I hardly know you, but…"

"Yes?" Krantz smiled encouragingly.

"Since this…thing happened, I had no one to talk to. My aunt, you know…she doesn't really understand a number of things."

"You want to talk to me? That's all right, you know. I will listen."

"I feel funny about this," Hubert continued. "As you know, I grew up in Germany, but I'm no longer used to these rules. These stages of warming up, from *Sie* to *Du*. After all, we've just been introduced to each other."

"I'm telling you, it's quite all right. Besides, I'm used to that," Krantz said.

"Used?"

"With the parents of the kids in my class. You don't know what kind of mess is going on in these houses. Behind those neat flower boxes and curtains." Krantz held his hands in front of himself, palms down, and made scrambling movements with his fingers, as though sifting through a muddy substance. He then pointed his index finger at Hubert.

"Shoot," he said, leaning back in his chair. "My name is Peter, by the way."

"Hubert. Just call me Hubert." A stream of words came out of him. He had been through his second glass of schnapps.

"I'm not ready for this. I used to live in this haze… There were always infinite possibilities, you know. A few weeks ago, this woman broke up with me—we'd spent only a few days together. She is vibrant, brilliant… Has it ever happened to you that you think of the time you spent with a woman as everything you ever wanted from life? It's a crazy feeling, and later you look back on your actions as though they were the actions of a stranger. Anyway, it was pretty difficult to go on from there. At least, that's what I thought at the time. Now all that seems so remote. And in a way so… silly."

He looked at Krantz to get some assurances to go on. Krantz nodded. He had comfortably settled in his chair and stretched his legs out. His face was open; he was clearly listening.

"You want me to tell you about her?"

Krantz nodded. Hubert told him about his attempts to bring some order into his life, about Helga long ago, about his disastrous marriage, about Helga in Scheveningen. His throat felt tight. Before he knew what was happening, he was shaken by sobs; an unknown force compressed his chest. He felt a needling pain marking the precise outline of his heart, as though his most vital organ was about to be rejected by his body.

"Peter, I… I can't live like this. You understand?" Hubert said with a hoarse voice.

Krantz shifted around in his seat.

"Hubert," he said. "Now look."

But this was as far as he got. It was clear that he didn't quite know how to proceed.

"I can't. I can't go on like this," Hubert said.

"Now look," Krantz said again. "From what Frieda tells me, you are a famous scientist."

"Famous or not, what good is it for now? You are talking about the past. What is the future going to be like? I mean, you could say a theoretician really needs nothing except books and a pencil and a scratchpad. But that is an image that is only true for illustrious minds like Einstein or Dirac. My more pedestrian kind needs colleagues, points of reference, daily motivation. And on top of this, I happen to be in a field that needs the computer for simulations."

Thus, Krantz had given him a new focus of argument, a rallying point for his senses. Hubert was composed again, but now he looked at his visitor with some apprehension. Krantz had seen him weak and in this funny state.

As if he had guessed what went through Hubert's mind, Krantz stepped forth and put his hand on Hubert's shoulder.

"You can trust me. I know how you feel," he said.

"Thanks," Hubert said, clasping his hand. He was touched by the efforts of his new friend to console him.

Krantz excused himself; he had to go to the bathroom. Hubert's mind drifted: *could he really write a textbook on fluid dynamics using the resources of the Innsbruck Hofbibliothek? A fantastic possibility, but how to get a publisher interested? Or should he see his accident (for this was the way he perceived his new condition: as the result of a freak accident; the wrong virus entering his respiratory tract at a time of fatigue, perhaps because he'd turned his head this way not that way during the conversation with a stranger on the train; he remembered the draft in the compartment after the window was opened and the old man who'd landed on his lap, whose mind was still infected with the century's worst pestilence) as a chance to leave science altogether, to pursue the form of quickthought lists and create an entirely new brand of literature? (Not publishable; too esoteric! Review headlines: "A quack Joyce in the Alps," "Scheveningen confused with Dublin," "Garbage treatment in the Netherlands: a topic of serious literature?" And where would he recruit his followers?) More down to earth, perhaps he could start a mail-order catalog for wooden shoes (bring a piece of flatland into the Alps. Good thinking! But would anybody care?). Or what about a gourd farm in Heilsheim? (An art of making money that had yet to be disproved!).*

"Hey, let's go to *Zum Hirschen*, have a beer," Krantz' said as he stepped back into the door.

"*Zum Hirschen*—To the Stag. I've heard about this place," Hubert said. "But isn't it uphill from here?"

"So what? I'll just push you there."

* * *

Hubert sniffed the night air and looked at the sky above. The mountains were just shapes now, recognizable only by the way they interrupted the generous cast of the stars. To have someone take control of the chair and to be able to escape the confines of the house filled him with great joy. He took a deep breath; the air was sweet with the scent of alpine herbs.

"The place is owned by the mayor," Krantz said in a low voice. They had reached the restaurant, a small building on top of the hill to which a terrace was attached. Flower boxes, meticulously kept, ran along the balustrade, overflowing with geraniums and begonias. A lonely couple sat on the terrace, heads touching, looking at the stars.

"That's Ingrid from the butcher's shop and Hans from the Miller farm, outside the village," Krantz whispered. "She went out with this guy Helmut before. Hans doesn't even know this."

"Oh boy," Hubert said, acknowledging the privileged information with a smile. He took it as the beginning of an initiation into the subtleties of village life and a sign of trust, a token, perhaps, of a coming friendship.

As Hubert, in his contraption, was thrust through the swinging entrance doors of the restaurant, a sea of noisy voices turned completely calm. Through the mist of smoke, he saw many eyes turned toward him over steak and goulash dishes. Too late, he thought of his trick to make himself invisible, which had last succeeded when he had taken Helga to the Circus Theatre. He made a quick effort to relax his facial muscles, to produce the desired blend of blandness and idiocy in his expression that had never failed to deflect the attention of guards and doorkeepers. But then he realized that his trick would be ineffective when he was faced with a curious crowd of onlookers. He also had a sense that something else interfered with the magic: it was one thing to make his face and even his body temporarily elusive to the eyes of a beholder, but it would be quite another to dissolve an entire chrome-plated wheelchair into thin air.

"Good evening, everyone!" he managed to shout with a cheerful face. Leaning back, he then hissed at Krantz, who had brought him into this predicament:

"Get me in a corner somewhere, please! These people stare at me like buzzards."

The murmur arose again, the sounds of forks and knives hitting china returned, and all the curious eyes wandered off.

"What a beginning," Hubert said when they had made their way through the tables (*nobody had the decency to budge!*) and to the far end of the room.

CHAPTER 23

Hubert awoke to the sounds of church bells. He lay motionless in his bed, watching a colorful band of light on the wall in jittery motion: some of the early-morning beams of the sun were refracted by the beveled edge of the mirror. He remembered the first time he'd seen the unearthly brilliance of the spectrum as a little boy. It seemed then to promise the existence of another reality, much more magical than the tangible things in his room: the window with the blinds, which were pierced by a pencil of light, the wall onto which the little rainbow was projected, the chair on which his shirt and pants were neatly laid out, and his big, fresh-smelling featherbed. After he had completed his physics courses, each appearance of that band of light seemed little more than a textbook quotation, pointing to the curvy symbols of calculus. Now, all of a sudden, the sense of being at the border of another world had returned; he stared at the flickering apparition as though it carried precious secrets, as though it concealed the answers to the question why he should be lying here, in this predicament, in the front room of a tiny house on the outskirts of a village with a scant five hundred souls on the edge of the Austrian Alps.

When Aunt Frieda entered his room to invite him to breakfast, she was unusually festive. She wore a blue *Dirndl* costume that lifted her breasts into two neat half-spheres and accentuated the atmosphere of order and cleanliness emanated by her whole person. Hubert was startled by the smell of her perfume. It was a musty lavender layered with desert flower scent, the kind that came in tiny bottles and was sold at medieval craft fairs back home.

In the kitchen, as he sipped his coffee and watched Aunt Frieda scramble the eggs, he tried to figure out where he had smelled this scent before. Perhaps—perhaps all the way back when he was little and still living with his parents in Germany. There were black-and-white pictures showing resolute Frieda holding him as a baby in front of his parents' house. He tried to imagine what it would be like if he could remember the touch of her breasts.

"You probably wonder what the occasion is," Aunt Frieda said.

"What's the occasion? I meant to ask," Hubert said.

"Glad you asked. Because it's my name day."

"Oh," Hubert said. "What does that mean, though? What is it about?"

Aunt Frieda turned around, her egg-yolk-covered hands half-closed in midair, and looked at him with big, round eyes.

"You don't know what it means? It means I'm going to church to light a candle, and then I meet the others."

"The others?"

"Two friends with the same name day. It's Toni—you know Toni, of course—and Valerie, the redhead. You met her, didn't you? Anyway, we meet this day every year for *Kaffee und Kuchen.*"

"Wait a minute. One's named Toni and the other Valerie. I don't understand. If it's name day for the three of you, are you not supposed to have the same name? Am I missing something?"

"Hildegard. It's the middle name that counts. Anton Hildegard Obermeyer, for example. Anton is Toni, of course."

There was little-girl excitement in her voice when she mentioned Toni, and Hubert was ready to believe that it was Toni for whom she had sculpted her bosom into this classic shape; it was Aunt Frieda's anticipation of seeing him that gave this day the extra sheen.

Surely, the way this world was created meant there existed for each woman at least one man who would lay his eyes upon her. As far as Hubert knew, this amazing law made no exception with all the crooked-nosed, flat-bosomed, droopy-eyed, even toothless varieties of females on this wide earth. Yet Aunt Frieda—well, Aunt Frieda seemed a different species: she was an aunt foremost and seemed to exist entirely outside the world of sexuality. Hubert was unable to conceive of an angle of approach, a possible point of male view, from which she could appear desirable as a lover. *Forgive me, Aunt Frieda*, he mumbled in his head.

The doorbell rang, and Aunt Frieda answered the door.

"Something for you," she said as she returned. "A big package. Really big. You have to sign."

Hubert heard heavy footsteps in the hallway and then a man's bass voice: "Where do you want this piece to go?"

Aunt Frieda stood next to Hubert as he signed his name.

"Wait," she hollered in the direction of the delivery man. And she turned back toward Hubert, asking, "What on earth is this? Where do you want me to put it?"

"I don't have the slightest idea," he said. "I didn't expect anything."

"But where is it from?" she asked.

"Holland. Apparently…" He studied the document. "Apparently, it's been sent to my hotel in Scheveningen and forwarded here. And it comes from a company called Zeewerken. Strange. Never heard of it."

"*Gnä Frau*, we've got to move on," one of the broad-shouldered men said as he appeared in the doorway, still in a servile pose.

"All right," she said. "Leave it in the hallway. Is it heavy?"

"It's light. Kind of bulky, though," the bulky man replied.

The package, as it turned out, contained a professional Class IV surfboard made from white reinforced polyester. The name of the model was California Sky. Next to the Zeewerken logo—the profile of a huge wave about to engulf a wheel—appeared three seagulls flying with wings spread wide and beaks open. The letter enclosed said: "*Congratulations! You have won the second prize in the Annual Waterfront Raffle. His Excellency, the Mayor of Scheveningen is pleased to present you the second prize with his compliments. May the surfboard keep you young and elastic as long as you live.*"

Hubert and his aunt looked at the surfboard with awe, as if nothing less than a whale had been stranded in the house. Aunt Frieda finally broke the silence.

"There are some lakes around here. It's not entirely off base, you know," she said, anxiously looking for signs of his reaction.

"Let's be realistic," Hubert said with a groan. "The idea of a surfboard in the Alps is bad enough. But a surfboard in *my hands* is a joke."

"Let's see. It could… it could be used as an ironing board," the ever-practical aunt suggested.

"No way. Polyester melts. Polyester burns."

"We could put flowers on it!"

And so it was decided. The board was propped up on two piles of cement bricks by the window in Hubert's room. It supported three pots of geraniums. The first fit perfectly on the wheel of the logo, the second pot shared the curve of the right wing with one of the birds, and the third pot was placed on an area free of designs, mostly for reasons of gravitational balance.

After Aunt Frieda left, already late for her middle-namesakes' outing, Hubert looked at the arrangement from the doorway. The surfboard, with its computer-designed, streamlined edges, bore a likeness to the kidney tables that had been in fashion when he'd been a teenager. As he gazed at the geraniums and their newly arrived support, he felt the grip of time, but also the presence of a peculiar inertia that seemed to afflict all physical things that mattered in his life.

CHAPTER 24—Aunt Frieda

T he day started like any day, with the sensation of pain in her knuckles. The sky was blue-gray, just bright enough to make out the contours of the snow-covered mountains. *So much snow this past winter!* A rooster crowed; it was the Tutzingers', next door. Aunt Frieda smiled. She liked the ragged sound; it reminded her of the time when she'd kept chickens herself. Five years ago, she'd given up on that, when her arthritis had started to bite. The Tutzingers' rooster was a fierce, strong-willed devil. *There! Listen! There is his mad crowing again!*

There was no healthy man in her house, yet there was so much to do! She kept the house clean, and she scrubbed the wooden floors. That was a woman's job. *But think of the stable! The work in the garden!* That past winter, the fence had collapsed under the weight of the snow.

(She remembered the day, past spring, when the Föhn, that warm alarming wind, had descended and consumed the snow in a single afternoon. When the snow melts so quickly with the sun's help, it becomes porous. Little needles form that point at the sun. *Take me, take me,* they seem to say. Later, when the snow has gone, the mud still remembers: it is covered with little knobs where the needles have been).

She had felt so helpless seeing the poles of the collapsed fence stuck into the air at odd angles, like in a giant's game of Mikado. Neighbors commiserated with her, standing around in the mud of the backyard. She had tears in her eyes that would not go away. The Tutzinger Maria was there, wearing boots, trying to ease her lot with little jokes. The rooster had followed Maria, pecking at things in the mud.

Aunt Frieda thought it was good to have neighbors who could share the bad things with her along with the good. But she couldn't help thinking they talked behind her back. What would they talk about? That she deserved it, of course. Twenty years ago, she'd married Paul, who'd grown up here. Black-mustached Paul! He had yodeled himself into her heart. She still remembered the way his body moved when they'd danced. It had been difficult for her to move to that Austrian village from the big town in Germany. The marriage had lasted precisely a year and eight weeks. After that, they'd agreed on one thing only: that they were not made for each other. Paul had stayed long enough to spread gossip about her and then taken a job as a waiter in Vienna. She'd lost track of him a long time ago.

(Kiikerikii! Again that wonderful sound!)

That was twenty years ago. Now she had to deal with the stories mothers had told their daughters who'd been babies then. A village in this part of the world had a long memory. As a person who'd moved here within the memory of the older villagers, she was supposed to show some humbleness for wrecking a marriage. Keeping her head up was interpreted as obstinacy. She would have to serve penance for another twenty years before she might be accepted as an equal.

Then Toni the carpenter had come along. *Strong, handsome Toni!* He'd fixed the fence in one frantic day. She still had the sound of his hammering in her ear. He hadn't fixed the gate that day. The week after that, he'd come with the gate but said he'd forgotten the hinges. And the next day, he'd brought the hinges and a bunch of flowers but had forgotten all about the lock and the bolts. So it was Toni almost every day, sitting in the kitchen, laughing, telling stories. It was as if the house had lit up. He was a respectable man with a respectable job. His wife had died a few years before.

Aunt Frieda spent her days holding her breath. Surely, one of these days, he would discover that her skin was wilting. Her hair had turned the color of straw. Looking at herself in the mirror, she was certain her body was shrinking. When she sat in the kitchen, she found herself putting her hands into fists to make the skin as taut as it used to be. But Toni had this inexplicable persistence, this *Dickköpfigkeit*—hard-headedness—in pursuing her. *Was he blind? Love was said to make people blind.* She blushed even thinking about Toni and her and what the books called love.

Aunt Frieda opened the heavy door leading from the kitchen to the stable and switched the light on. She walked into the sharp, warm smell of goat and heard the rustling of Karoline in the straw.

"Good girlie," she said. "Time to get up. *Morgenstund hat Gold im Mund*—Morning hour, golden flower."

She stroked the animal's head between the ears. The goat stiffened her body and leaned against Aunt Frieda's touch. Her green slit-eyes stared at her as though much bigger eyes were peeking through a fence. Her brown udder swung this way and that, heavy from last night's accumulation of milk. It was really enough milk for two, but Hubert, shortly after arriving, had drunk a glass of it and expressed disgust.

"Like piss," he'd said. "Like lukewarm goddamn piss."

"Hubert!" she remembered herself reprimanding him. "Filthy words like that in *my* house!" Her nephew was such a difficult, choleric man. Sometimes after an argument, she went into her bedroom and cried. She'd always envied her sister for having a son. Now that she'd inherited her sister's son, she found his presence overbearing. There now was a man in the house all right, but it was not the type of man she'd thought of. The extra pair of hands were pretty much tied up. And he seemed like a little child, spoiled and contrary. She was trying to decide if it had to do with his disability. If she took away his brashness, his impatience, was there somewhere (albeit hidden) a pot of gold? How different things might have been if he hadn't caught that virus!

With a sigh, she shoved the clean galvanized bucket underneath the goat, sat down on her three-legged milking stool, and readied her rosy hands for the zig-zag work that must be done every day.

CHAPTER 25

When Hubert awoke, there was a curious smell in the room. It was not unpleasant, but it was hard to place. He decided it could be some kind of fruit. He looked around in his room and—voila!—found a large bag filled with apples on his table. They were red-speckled, rather small. *Aunt Frieda, the good soul! She must have tiptoed into his room while he was asleep. But how could she think he could eat so many of them? At the rate of an apple a day, the bag would last him until Christmas. God no, by Christmas he wanted to be back home! There was no way he could keep that whole bag.*

But then he saw the rest. Next to the bag with the apples lay two knives on a cutting board: a sharp knife to quarter and core the apples and a peeling knife to do the rest. On the floor beneath his desk there were two large cooking pots. For a second Hubert stared at the invasion of kitchenware. "This is… she wants me to…," he mumbled. And then it became clear to him that she was asking him to put in his share of work. But why would she be so sneaky about this? Why not ask him directly? Or leave a note, at least!

The apples had been picked by Toni. Hubert had heard Toni and Aunt Frieda's voices in the backyard the day before. Their voices had sounded happy, like those of children. Once, he had seen the ladder being carried by the window. It hurt to see another man's strength displayed like that. And as far as the apples were concerned, she could've just asked *him* instead!

The apples were oddly shaped, products of a harsh climate. It seemed hardly worth peeling them: there wouldn't be much left once the core was removed. They had warts, wormholes, and bruises. One could imagine faces, especially in this pale early light of the day.

With the calmness of a man who is able to see ahead, he picked the first apple from the pile and looked at it from all sides. Yes, it was unmistakably Eric's face: there was his broad forehead, even something of his grin. It's me thinking of Eric that stacks up my senses, Hubert thought, fending off a feeling of awe. If I were hiking now, I'd be seeing him in a cloud. He looked at the other apples on top of the pile, turned them around one by one, and made sure they were all strangers. The world was in a whirling motion, always ordering and sorting and re-ordering a vast mass of things. He was, after all, a scholar of turbulence, a subject that would haunt him to the end of the world. There was no significance in coincidences without a recognizing, contemplating mind. Yet sometimes he wanted to believe in a sign. He wanted to believe he was being spoken to by something from somewhere out there.

He set his friend's likeness aside, on top of the typewriter, before he took the knife in his hand. He started cutting the second apple into quarters. As he peeled the quarters, the foamy sap ran over his fingers.

What he would give for a chat over beer with his friend!

* * *

As the weeks went by and the days grew shorter, Hubert watched the growth of a warm feeling inside. He watched it unfold like the seed of an unknown plant that had been carried by the wind to a crevice in the asphalt and taken root. The seed would start with two leaves that opened like a book written in a cryptic code. It revealed little about the forms encapsulated in the small bud sitting between the leaves. Then, after a few days, another pair of leaves would emerge—these now with definite shapes and complexions—and spur sudden recognition of a familiar tree: the zigzagged border of the hazelnut bush, the first tiny pentagon of the maple tree.

So it happened that one day, Hubert stopped himself in the middle of his morning chores. He suddenly realized what it was he had nourished: the hope of seeing Helga again after a period of heroic hardship. Or rather, it was more than hope: it was the anxious certainty that a child has who has lost sight of his mother. Of course, eventually, Helga would realize the foolishness of her action, would recognize the existential quality of an irreversible loss that could yet be avoided, and would rush back, if not in time, then at least in space, to re-occupy a place that was hers. Cosmologically preordained. That place was next to him. Certainly, all his struggles could not have been in vain; they were his advance payment in a convoluted bargain, a payment he was quite willing to give.

Paradoxically, the longer he waited for a letter, for a telephone call, a telegram, the more certain he grew of the one and only outcome. Every day began with Hubert awakening, listening for the crunching sounds of the mailman's footsteps in the snow. On most days, the footsteps came and went without approaching the door. On the few days when he heard the delicious sound—clank-clank—of mail being dropped in the wooden box outside, he rushed to the front door, propelling himself with swift movements of his hands (he had gotten so strong in his arms!). He would find the electricity bill, offers for the shipment of Burgundy wine, and an appeal to support the South Tyrolian Freedom Fighters in their struggle against their Italian usurpers, but no letter from her.

CHAPTER 26

Each day, the non-arrival of a letter from Helga was a major event. Christmas came and went, with all the decorum and kitsch the holiday commanded in the village, but still no letter. Snow fell in masses, 27 centimeters, 85 centimeters, a hundred and forty-five centimeters. Snow measured in centimeters was so much more than in measly inches. Snow as high as Aunt Frieda was tall. Nevertheless, there was no letter. Snow ploughs and snow blowers scraped and rattled and hummed. Weeks went by while the village lay asleep under a white coat glistening in the sun. Every day, hope of the crisp, hurting kind was dashed within the span of seconds when the mailman arrived (*a skimpy heap of mail without promise! Why did he even bother to stop by! Those disappointing domestic stamps! The pedantic-looking format of Austrian business letters!*).

That hope was followed by hope of another kind that was not so easily discouraged, as it drew from a deeper well. Obviously, Helga was taking longer still (*perhaps just one more day?*) to make up her mind. He knew her as a strong-willed person. Her kind needed patience and—in advance—forgiveness. Generosity was called for, not swiftness of judgment. Yet sometimes he also found himself working on a lecture he would give her, scolding her for all the letters unwritten to her mother, her two nieces, her best friend who had moved to England; for her failure, in one word, to sit down on her little ass and invest five minutes of her life into doing what needed to be done, *goddammit!* "But they know me!" she would always defend herself. "They don't mind."

He was struck by the irony of it: knowing her, he should expect with certainty *not* to get a letter from her, perhaps ever. Thus, in a way, the absence of Helga's letter each morning made her presence more strongly felt: it was a greeting of sorts, admittedly amorphous and indirect, yet perhaps not less passionate than any positive evidence of thinking of him, of love.

Aunt Frieda watched the early-morning ritual with apparent amusement.

"She must be quite a girl," she said one day early in March.

"She's quite a girl for sure," he replied, blushing; somehow his aunt's generous remark had invited Helga into this pastoral scene and promptly conjured the image in his mind of his girlfriend jogging, crossing the entire length of the village, from the schoolhouse to the bakery, clad in earrings, a fine silver chain around her ankle. *And nothing else.*

It was not long after that—April 4, an indelible date—when an envelope bearing her scribbly handwriting arrived. It felt thick and heavy in his hands when he pulled it out of the box. He stared at the package for a few seconds without moving. It had been postmarked in Stuttgart. He looked around. The morning air was fresh; the Hundertzack was still the color of a velvety-black with pink on which the snow sat like whipped cream on a piece of *Sachertorte.*

The day Helga's letter arrived had started so innocently, so understated, that it made perfect sense. Hubert swallowed hard. There was a metallic taste in his mouth. *No, it had to be a joke. Surely, someone had played a trick on him. The handwriting was too perfectly Helga's. Aunt Frieda? The good soul, she wouldn't, couldn't possibly... but Victor! It had to be one of his practical jokes. Victor, you bastard! But who among his friends knew that Stuttgart was her present domicile? Yet there was the joyful possibility, after all, that the letter had really come straight from her.*

Hubert hastened to get back into his room, past the kitchen where Aunt Frieda was waiting with his coffee and the daily hard-boiled egg. He cherished the delicious weight of the letter—it was a package, almost— but he also anxiously recalled her "final" letter in Scheveningen, which had refused to change its contents when he'd used his magical powers of wishing. He locked his door, took a deep breath, and opened the envelope. What he found was a stack of photographs wrapped in a piece of paper bearing a note:

Dear Hubert:

Some housecleaning. I didn't know what to do with them. I thought you might want them back. Hope you are well.

Love, Helga.

He stared at the pictures without comprehension. "Didn't know," he mumbled. "What to do. Want them back. House-cleaning. I thought. You might. He, she, it did. Didn't know. Didn't clean. Didn't want. Didn't hope. Didn't love!"

He made his hands into fists and drummed on his desk, accompanying his staccato declension. After a few seconds, there was a knock on the door.

"Hubert? Are you all right?" he heard Aunt Frieda say as the door handle moved.

"Please stay out. Please leave me alone. This is *my* room!" Hubert shouted.

There was silence on the other side of the door and then the sound of quick, resolute steps moving away. For a while, he heard the sounds of pots and pans banging in the kitchen. Slowly he raised one of the photographs to his eyes. It showed him and Helga standing hand in hand in front of one of the giant planters that flanked the entrance of Aan Zee. He remembered the freckle-faced teenage boy they'd asked to take their picture.

"This bitch," he said. "I can't believe it, this bitch."

Hubert had to go to the bathroom, past the open kitchen door. As he was wheeling by, Aunt Frieda stepped out, her eyes piercing.

"Hubert, you owe me an apology," she said, her voice almost toneless.

"I didn't mean it," he said. His bladder hurt.

"That's not good enough."

"I didn't mean to say it, for Christ's sake. It's about her. I got this letter and some photographs."

"What does the letter say?"

"Nothing. She waits months and months, and then—nothing! As though we'd never met."

"You poor boy!" Aunt Frieda said, stepping closer.

"Let me just go to the bathroom," he pleaded, escaping her motherly embrace.

When he returned, Aunt Frieda stood at his desk. She had the photographs in her hands like a deck of cards.

"She *is* beautiful," she said.

"You just went into my room and got the pictures from my desk," Hubert said slowly. "This is not OK. You understand this, Aunt Frieda? It's not OK."

"You look like a perfect couple," she said in a simple voice.

"Give them back to me. At once. You have no business in my room."

"Ungrateful boy!" his aunt exclaimed, her eyes fired up. "I clean every morning; I open the windows; I put the bed things on the windowsill for fresh air; I check if you still have enough Tempo napkins on your nightstand. I cook your food every day and serve it to you right here. To sum it up once and for all: I do have a lot of business in your room."

She stormed out. Hubert was shaking. Something had to be done. There was just no way to live like this: it felt like being under an old spinster's microscope.

CHAPTER 27

There it was again, the chime of the hour, the chime of the near future, the chime of the never-ending story. Aunt Frieda's clock reached out to strike his eardrum, striking without mercy the five hundred billion dendrites, the gray matter, the corpus callosum, the convoluted lobes of his brain. Hubert contemplated his misfortune, scribbling:

> *The first clocks, centuries ago, were portents of astronomy; they revolved in synchrony with the planet; they brought a touch of eternal order to the castles and mansions of the aristocracy. Later, in many forms, the timepiece invaded the homes of the burghers; it came to stand for constancy and order. Out of this divine instrument, the Swiss made a pedantic contraption, a little cathedral of monotony.*

Aunt Frieda's clock had a little platform upon which a deer family made its appearance every hour. Following a strict patriarchal order, the imposing *Zwöelfender* was the first to make the rounds: he appeared in a roaring pose with his mouth open and his head raised, upon which his twelve-pronged antlers were planted. The expression and furtherance of triumph seemed his sole purpose. He was followed by his narrow-shouldered, pristine-hipped female companion and their cute, high-legged, big-eyed Disney World offspring. Once the threesome had emerged from a hole in the papier-mâché underbrush, a chime started to sound to mark the hour. It was followed by the voice of an invisible cuckoo. The deer family briefly contemplated the formal furniture they had seen some sixty-thousand times, and then disappeared into a hole symmetrically placed with respect to hole number one.

The cuckoo is having a go at eternity. Another year of listening to this bird, and I'd be a hundred years old. By that time, I'd be too old to act on impulse. Impulse, indeed, would compel me right now to take a two-by-four and whack the box and make this bird homeless once and for all.

From the moment his body became more confined, Hubert's mind had sought opportunities to escape. He had come to dread all recurring events because they suggested standstill, making him feel as though his very thoughts were being strapped to some type of orthopedic device. So, to Hubert, the clock that was Aunt Frieda's faithful companion soon became an instrument of torture. In an attempt to evade its hourly demands on his ears, he kept his radio playing at high volume. She seemed to regard his act of defense as a willful provocation, so when she entered his room, she went straight for his stereo amplifier, not looking left nor right, to adjust the emerging wattage to levels she was willing to accept.

There's time, and again, there's time. There are good times and bad times and all kinds of times that fall in between. There are past times and past tenses, and then, folks, here's something heavy: the future. The future is tense, the past is gone, and the present is elusive like a mailman who has spotted a Doberman. We know this. We can live with this. But with a loudmouthed cuckoo-clock, things get scrambled. The past is the future, and before you know it, the future is gone. With this hysterical timepiece, you can only shred time into pieces too small to pick up, too small to do anything with. Who is this inventor, this Hoerli or Muesli or Gruetzimitanand? What did he intend to do to mankind?

Gears—yes, that was it! He needed to introduce gears, gearshifts, and electrical propulsion. What a paradox to behold: that he would need to make a clockwork out of his wheelchair to escape the curse of time. The village was laid out on a hill, and the roads were steep and inaccessible to his weak, hand-powered contraption. It took him a few phone calls to find out that the price of freedom was well outside his budget. He wrote an urgent letter to Eric:

Dear Eric!

The circumstances of my life have drastically changed. At some point, I will find the time to explain. Right now, my financial situation is bleak. What it boils down to is I need cash. I lent you a total of 10 grand to help you get started with your green munchkins. Given the shaky nature of your enterprise (not a reflection of your skills and determination as a businessman, don't get me wrong!) I didn't expect to see much profit, to begin with. Right now, I'm not talking about profit or even interest. I just need the money back. Please be quick. Wire it.

—your friend Hubert.

He added the name of his local branch, the local Farmer's Alliance, and the number of the account.

* * *

"There's a lot of superstition in this area," Peter Krantz said after finishing his tea. He was on his afternoon visit to Aunt Frieda's house on his way home from school. As usual, he had arrived at precisely five minutes after three.

"About what?" Hubert asked.

"About lots of things. There are all kinds of cures for everything. Me, I don't believe a bit of what these people say."

"Cures? Like, for cancer?"

"Sure. A mixture of gentian and sage and *Wohlgemut.* You grind the plants up, boil them, let them simmer. And you have to drink the stuff at the time of the full moon," Peter chuckled.

"Full moon, eh? Tell me, what do they say about...this?" Hubert padded the small of his back with his hand.

"I don't know," Peter said, his eyes shifting.

"Tell me what you think. There is something you don't want to tell me about."

"It's too...far-fetched, crazy."

"Peter!" Hubert pleaded. "You brought up the subject of cures."

"All right. I'll tell you. But don't you complain afterward. They say… they say people who are lovesick like you…"

"Lovesick like me? Who on earth told them? Who the hell told them about my love affairs?" Hubert exploded.

"It's a village. You know this kind of village. Things get around. You know you can't hide a thing from a small place like this."

"What do they do? Put my letters over steam before they go out? I want to talk to the mailman—what's his face?"

"Rudi? Jesus, calm down, he wouldn't do anything to your letters. Rudi, of all people!"

"If it isn't Rudi, then who else?" Hubert continued, his anger still rising. "Is it my aunt? Are you saying that in a village like this, I can't even *think* without being spied on?"

"It's just small; that's all I said. For all I know, they might be watching your face too closely. Your face sure tells a lot."

"So, what do they say about me being lovesick?"

"They think something in you just gave up."

"Aha. And do they have a cure?"

"They say—this is really funny!—what they say is that in the state you're in, to get cured, you have to lie with a woman." Peter laughed nervously and started rubbing his nose.

"Is this what you think, too?" Hubert asked. He stared at his visitor with rage.

"Me? Me, believe in that type of garbage?" Peter replied. He pulled a white handkerchief out of his pocket to rub his nose some more. There was an awkward pause.

Hubert continued: "I resent this. You know, I really resent being pitied. I resent your telling me this kind of idiotic gossip. You are doing this because you are just like the others: people with sick fantasies. *'Lie with a woman!'* That figures. In your fantasy, I'm this desperate product of fate. I'm this lonely cripple who can't get through a single night without self-abuse. I've gone limp for good—that's what you all think—and there is nothing else on my mind, for all you know, but to lie with a woman! For the record, I'm perfectly all right. This is a different way of spending my day from the way I was used to, but it's decent, dignified, fulfilled."

Hubert had talked himself into a rage. Peter raised his hands as if trying to stem an invisible tide, but to no avail.

"They used it to cure syphilis, you know?" Hubert went on. "Have you read *The Great Train Robbery*? The blood of a virgin freshly deflowered. Now, there I could see a glimpse of a plausible mechanism, at least: innocence, by its sheer power, flushing away the morbid germs of another body. (Here Hubert waved his hands dramatically, like Moses parting the sea.) But how in the world can lying with a woman affect my spine? Is this some kind of chiropractic lovemaking your village wisdom has in mind? Position eight hundred and nine: he lies on his stomach, and she jumps on his ass from a high altitude. Let's see... the dresser! The dresser might be the right height."

Hubert had started wheeling in a zigzag through the room, no longer with his eyes focused on Herr Krantz, but looking right through him, as though he had recognized some pattern of generic, ubiquitous evil. Peter looked uncomfortable. He inched back toward the door as Hubert went on:

"And then crack, it says, the quintessential crack that is music to the ears of the chiropractor, the cracking sound that restores the harmony of disk assembly and is followed by a wave of soothing pain. Crack, then it says as the virgin lands on the patient-lover's back. The key is turned, the spine re-connects, the muscle flexes, the prince emerges, the lover turns around on his own free will to embrace her and give her (that Indian giver!) the very gift she has set free."

There was a knock on the door. Aunt Frieda slipped in.

"*Mein Gott*, what is all that noise about?" she exclaimed.

"He is un-stop-able," Peter said, shrugging. He stressed each syllable of this word, as if giving the final verdict on a miscreant student. "He just goes on like this. I wished I could help him."

"Help me? Right. Why don't you ask my aunt to get me a nice girl? My type is blonde, narrow-hipped, firm-breasted, with an ass like a knockwurst."

"Stop this talk in my house right now!" Aunt Frieda stomped her foot. Her eyes sparkled with anger and indignation. "Nothing but trouble from the day you stepped into my house."

"I was carried in," Hubert crowed, triumphant about the opportunity to have the last word in this matter.

"I guess I better go," Peter said.

"Oh... could you take... this letter to the mailbox?" Hubert said, suddenly feeling awkward. Without another word, Peter took the letter, turned on his heels, and left the room.

There was a long, terrible silence in the room. Aunt Frieda rearranged the flowerpots on the surfboard. Hubert rubbed his forehead and then scratched his ear. He tried to understand how he'd gotten into the frenzy. He wished he were alone.

"You should be ashamed of yourself," Aunt Frieda finally said.

"He said things that hurt so much," Hubert said. "I'll call him tomorrow. But what you said, 'nothing but trouble,' is that really what you think?"

"Hubert, dear, one says things if one is excited."

"Aunt Frieda, you've got to tell me, OK? I don't want to be anyone's trouble."

"Hubert, I wish I hadn't said it. I really don't mind at all. It's like... having a kid in the house to care for. It feels good."

After she left, Hubert sat motionless in his room as the dusk arrived. He looked at his white hand. He looked at his fingers as he moved them one by one. They looked like strange animals grafted onto his body. He thought of one question: how is it possible to speak and think at the same time?

CHAPTER 28

"**D**iscreet dancing for your private needs," the advertisement said. Hubert was leafing through the *Wiener Woche*, the weekly entertainment guide of Vienna, when he found these electrifying words. Surely, "private needs" went with private parts; discreet dancing could only mean indiscreet display of a body in motion; and the word "your" clearly referred to him. Hubert immediately knew what was to be done. It was Sunday. On Tuesday morning, Aunt Frieda was going to have an appointment with the hairdresser. Hubert anxiously awaited the hour when he would have the phone by himself. His heart sank when she stayed in bed a good part of Monday and complained of headaches and a stuffy nose. But the next morning, he heard the sounds of her early chores in the kitchen and instantly knew that his plan was safe. The minute she left the house, Hubert wheeled into the hallway and dialed the number. A woman named Ilana answered the phone. She had a slight Slavic-sounding accent, perhaps Czech? Her voice was full and promising, and he asked her to take a taxi to Heilsheim. She was incredulous. How could she be sure he'd pay for the ride? He told her only then that he was handicapped, and given this predicament, what reason would he have to stiff her? That did the trick, and she finally agreed.

The day for the intimate dance was set for Friday, Aunt Frieda's regular day to go to the market. On that day, she usually took the bus to the district's capital and came back late. As much as he despised her clock-like performance, he had to admit to himself that he had come to rely on the resulting programmed privacy. He knew what he was planning now was so far beyond her comprehension that he could not ask for her permission. To silence a persistent nagging inner voice, he told himself that he was simply forced by the unusual circumstances to break his aunt's trust.

Hubert spent the days in nervous anticipation. He listened to Ilana's voice in his memory, trying to imagine her face and her build. In his mind, she took shape as a brunette with the radiant smile and crisp breasts of a cheerleader. Once, a member of this species had appeared at his doorstep back in the US and overwhelmed him with a pitch on nuclear waste. While she had gone on a great length about dangers and the half-lives of elements, he had stared at her as though she were an apparition straight from a netherworld between heaven and hell. From the bottom of her white miniskirt—unbearable and improbable suggestion of innocence!—there had emerged brown legs so perfectly sculpted that he'd emitted an involuntary moan and had needed to force his hands behind his back. It was this college girl from Oneonta who shed her brassiere five hundred thousand times in his dreams and half-awake states: his cesium and strontium Madonna. Ilana had sounded like this, and the light Slavic accent hinted at a woman who, once inflamed, would know no limits.

He expected her arrival at four o'clock in the afternoon. He'd set the time so early to make the maximum use of Aunt Frieda's absence. The hour came and went with no taxi in sight. Hubert roamed through the house, tapping on the walls, opening and closing the refrigerator, combing his hair in front of the bathroom mirror for the third time. Finally, at six, he heard the tuck-tuck-tuck sound of a Mercedes diesel. The sun was about to disappear behind the Hundertzack, letting the valley sink into a giant blue shadow. Looking out of his window, he observed a blonde woman emerge from the car, still immersed in the sunlight. She wore a mink coat (*it had to be false!*) over a blue dirndl dress with pink flowers running up and down and walked on unsteady high heels clearly made to be worn in barrooms. The two ends of her red scarf fluttered in the light breeze. She carried a brown crocodile leather bag, which Hubert, behind his curtain, presumed to contain the requisites of her trade.

From where he was sitting, at least, Ilana looked pretty. As she moved, she swung her hips in an exaggerated way. Her very exit from the Mercedes looked as though planned as part of a performance. Hubert greeted her at the front door.

"Sorry I'm late," she said with her full melodic voice, now modulated with the higher timbres that never come across on the phone. "But this fucking cab had a flat."

"What's the matter with you?" she continued, pointing at his wheelchair. "Do you have to stay in this thing?"

"I'll explain in a minute," Hubert said.

Having allowed a brief grace period for this introduction, the taxi driver, a bear of a man wearing a mustache and lederhosen with suspenders, got out of the car and asked for his money. Hubert produced a bill, but Ilana stepped between the two men and asked how exactly, *bitteschön,* she would get back to Vienna?

"Don't you worry," Hubert managed to say. "There is a pension here, Pension Walther. They always have a room. And in the morning, no problem at all, you can take the nine o'clock express bus, which stops a few minutes from here."

Seeing that Ilana was satisfied with the plan, the driver took the money but left with a confused look in his eyes.

After the tuck-tuck-tuck of the diesel had faded out behind the hills, she faced Hubert fully. Her skin was white and porous.

"So, this is the place," she said. "Neat. How many people are you expecting?"

"How many people?" Hubert asked, gasping.

"You asked me to strip, right? Where are the people? I need an audience to strip to."

"It's just me. You understand? I thought I told you that. It's just for me."

"Oh boy," she said. Apparently, it was her turn now to be surprised. "For one single guy? I've never done that before. And hands off my tits; that needs to be understood."

Hubert asked her to step into the house. She stumbled slightly, adjusting herself to the sudden darkness of the hallway. She caught her balance by grasping Hubert's shoulder as he reeled ahead. Upon impulse, Hubert tilted his head to brush her arm.

"I'm fucking starved," she said. "I know this is unprofessional, asking for stuff like that, but do you have a thing to eat before I get into action?"

He invited her to sit down at the freshly scrubbed maple wood table and wheeled himself to the pantry. For his convenience, Aunt Frieda had arranged the most important food items on a single shelf within easy reach. Looking back at the table, seeing a young blonde woman with makeup occupying Aunt Frieda's place underneath the picture of her parents, his grandparents, he suddenly knew that he would not be forgiven. His transgression was grave beyond comprehension; within the century it had been standing, this house had not seen sin and sacrilege of this kind. He was filled with a mixture of shame and pride. It was the shame of a guest who recognizes his abuse of hospitality and the pride of a gambler who loves to take credit for the high risks he has been willing to take.

Ilana made some tea, and in the end, she had her elbows on the table, slowly pivoting her cup between her hands, just like Aunt Frieda did every night before she went to bed. Hubert wheeled into the living room and lit three candles. Outside, the blue shadow of the mountains had turned a dark, velvety brown. Ilana put her dishes into the sink and retreated into the bathroom, presumably to open her crocodile leather bag and don the lightweight lingerie soon to be shed again. She reappeared in a slippery thing that was carmine red and bordered by black lace. It barely covered the penumbrae of her nipples. She asked for music to dance to, and Hubert complied by selecting a tape of a slow waltz, which he inserted into his portable tape recorder with shaking hands.

Leaning back in his wheelchair, he saw Ilana and the ballet of the three flickering shadows she cast on the walls. Her movements were like those of a child: clumsy but deeply earnest. Now and then, almost carelessly, she shed a piece of her clothes. She stripped without teasing, never taking her eyes off Hubert. In the darkness, and blinded by the candles, Hubert saw little more than the undulating silhouette of her body. Staring at the shape that floated in front of him, he finally saw geometric figures that were a shade darker still: the two perfect circles of her nipples and the precise triangle of her pubic hair. These highly loaded geometric figures chased one another, exchanged places, or stood almost still in a vibrating motion. Hubert felt all fluids of his body come awake; he closed his eyes for seconds, trying to imagine and remember what he'd just seen with his eyes open. Then he opened his eyes again to compare what he'd just imagined with the real thing.

"Ilana," he said with a hoarse voice. "Come and touch me."

But instead, she put her finger on her lips, motioning him to keep silent. She moved away from him so that her body was half-immersed in the light of the candles. Different parts of her body emerged from the darkness like phases of the moon. Hubert found himself crying. *It was all so futile!* The watching created the urge to touch, the touching the desire to unite bodies, yet once united, the bodies were still not content but strived for the impossible: the complete, unconditional fusion of the souls. *What is love in the final analysis but utter torture!*

Ilana seemed to sense his distress; she came near and stroked his hair, still moving along with the slow waltz. Hubert pressed his head against her arm in the manner of a cat. Her small adolescent breasts were now close to his eyes. He marveled about the comprehensive list of services included in her fee. She had brewed him a cup of tea, stripped for him, danced for him alone in the nude, and now managed to play his mother! Could there be more? He did not dare imagine it.

There were noises at the window. Giggling? Could it be? In the darkness of the glass, where the curtains of the window left a gap, Hubert saw two pale apparitions—the faces of two kids—this much he could make out. Ilana emitted a shriek and hid behind a chair while Hubert gesticulated towards the window, his face contorted with anger. The faces disappeared, but now the room seemed to have lost its sheen. Ilana crawled back from her hiding place.

"Could we call the pension now? I'm dead tired," she said.

There was no answer at the pension. Incredulous, Hubert let the phone at the other end ring for three minutes and then shook his head.

"I don't understand. They're always there."

"You mean there's no room for me? *Himmel, Arsch, und Zwirn,"*— "Goddamn Motherfucking Shit!," she screamed, crouched over her brown suitcase. "This pisses me off, you know. You told me it's all set."

"Don't worry. You're welcome to sleep here on the couch. Nothing to fear from me, ha, ha. No need to be bashful either; I've seen you without clothes already, after all."

"Shit. Shit-shit-shit! You knew it all along! Pay me now, or I call the pigs!"

After Hubert gave her the money, Ilana disgruntledly agreed to stay. She spent a minute in the bathroom to put her see-through nightgown on, still swearing, and then curled up on the couch like a cat, without saying goodnight. He looked at his watch. It was only ten o'clock. Aunt Frieda wasn't expected back until eleven. She would go to sleep right away, get up at 5:30 in the morning to feed the animals and milk the goat, and then go to bed again to sleep in until nine. There would be no problem for Ilana to slip out undetected.

He watched her slim body move with the breathing of deep sleep. She could well have been his daughter. He was relieved that she had fallen asleep before him and so was spared the sight of his awkward roll from the wheelchair into his bed. He was awake for a long time, listening to her breathing, admiring her trust in the world and the eminently practical way in which she was conducting her life. Somehow the crocodile leather bag, which now stood next to her, exemplified all that was mysterious and charming about her. It was all scratched up on the outside and was equipped with two tiny locks. The key was probably attached to a silver chain around her neck, nestled between her breasts, rising and falling with the gentle movement of her chest.

* * *

When he awoke, something warm stirred next to him; it was her: the perfume was unmistakably hers! Her body was rolled up next to his, and her mouth was on his groin, working its way down. He was convinced he was still dreaming, as in the many dreams before in which one dream was encased in others in the manner of Russian dolls. Something was telling him that a hooker from Vienna wouldn't be doing *this*. Pretending to be asleep, believing, in fact, that he dreamed to be pretending, he moved his hand and at once felt the touch of her thick, cool hair. So it was Ilana! He held his breath with excitement and then continued to breathe as if to ensure the uninterrupted progress of her head and mouth—dream or no dream. As he was restraining his hand from touching her breast, from exploring her body, he felt the firm tug of her lips and surrendered to a feeling long forgotten.

Without a sound, she slipped out from under the blanket, tiptoed toward her couch—he saw the precise outline of her torso against the light of dawn coming from the very window where the curious eyes had appeared a few hours earlier –and lay down once more to continue her sleep of innocence.

A dream, he concluded, would not go through the extraordinary trouble of fusing things into the kind of reality that might still be remembered in this state; a dream would just be sloppy toward the end: it might have had her wander off into the night, hungry and barefooted, or simply turn her into his aunt. Thus, he decided that he was thoroughly awake and that the miracle had not been merely conjectured but had really happened to him. He lay there in bliss, contemplating his unexpected fortune, still smelling her perfume and watching the light of dawn grow to become the light of the day.

* * *

Hubert awoke from a terrible commotion: the sound of the door bursting open, the high pitch of Frieda's voice in extreme excitement, the light of the early dawn seeping into the window. Slowly Hubert began to understand what it was she was screaming.

"Who's this person? Answer me! Who?"

He quickly looked at the couch: only a crumpled-up blanket marked the place where Ilana had slept.

"What person?" Hubert said, coughing. *My God! The smell of this cheap perfume is everywhere! I wished she'd had the decency to mop up this awful smell!*

"That woman. A woman just left. I saw her go," Frieda screamed. "Don't tell me I'm seeing things!"

Hubert had never seen her so agitated.

"Aunt Frieda," he said. "Listen. Sit down. You must be dreaming."

"Who is she? You dare to do this kind of thing in my house! You… slimebag. Believe me, without your wheelchair and all that, I swear I would kick you out right now."

"Gee," he snorted, "I'm really grateful I'm paralyzed. At least there's one thing good about it. It sure seems to curb the wrath of some people around here."

There was no denying it in the end. Underneath the blanket, Aunt Frieda found a red scarf whose sudden appearance Hubert could not explain. There were two tea bags in the kitchen sink *(True, he never drank two in a row. How petty those arguments would always get!)*. The ubiquitous eau de cologne! And when Aunt Frieda's temper had settled enough for Hubert to offer her some of his money toward the cost of her shopping, he opened his wallet and found that the money was gone.

CHAPTER 29—Ilana

Ilana felt out of place on the bus, with her false mink coat and her crocodile leather bag. The men stared at her knees, just below her skirt, as the bus tumbled along. There was absolutely nothing to see, and she let them see it, even helping her legs a bit to follow the movements of the carriage. The women stared at her bag, guessing the contents. She knew the ugly name they gave it, *Beischlafutensilienkoffer*—cohabitation utensil portmanteau, concatenated in one word all at once. Ignoring their stares, she opened it just wide enough to take out a nail file. She had plenty of time to kill.

What will I tell Michael, though?

"I danced for a handicapped scientist"? (He won't believe it.) "I stripped for a man in a wheelchair?" (He's gonna think this is hilarious.)

"I let him touch my pussy"? "I let his finger do the walking"? "I put a sign out: 'Slippery When Wet'"? (He's gonna roar with laughter!)

"I spread my legs for him to see"? (He'll say I hope you took a shower!) "I ate him while he was asleep"? (He's gonna get sick in his stomach.)

"I cleaned out his wallet"? (He would love it—but he's not gonna know!)

Hubert. Hubert who? Hubert the disabilitated American? Or is it disabled? Debilitated? A stranded, mysterious man of science. Action, reaction. Achtung! Reaktor! Cause and effect. Fuck and counterfuck. Donor and receptacle. Americans had big ones; that was a statistical fact. It was a feat of evolution. Survival of the longest. (Perhaps because the snatches of American women were retracting? A curious byproduct of feminism? Mr. Penis had to follow.) Long, big, and without that smelly, floppy piece of skin. God must've started making tails all over again over there. Women weren't supposed to notice the difference. Only whores spent their time obsessing about the sizes of dicks. Decent women just didn't care. What had turned her on was his helplessness. To be attached to a piece of meat like that, yet to be so immobilized!

"Turbulence is my profession," he'd said to her. What a weird thing to say! Fucking is mine, she now continued the conversation in her mind.

"What's turbulence?" she'd managed to say.

"Things in quick, quirky motion. Screwy, you might say."

Ah! Finally, a hint at the strong connection between his brain and his more basic functions. He could have been the one. The sound of his voice on the phone! The idea of someone paying for a seventy-five-kilometer cab ride just to see her dance! Whenever she took a cab to a new destination, this idea came back again of the hero, the final fuck. The final turbulent fuck would embrace the woman in her. She would follow her final fuck to the end of the world. He would be really sweet and hold her and not let go of her. There was a finality in being with him. Hearing Hubert's voice on the phone, she'd thought she had found that man.

She'd imagined packing her suitcase, this time for good. She imagined the final conversation with Michael, her pimp: *"Where do you think you are going?" –"None of your business, you creep."—"More than you think, my sweet slot!" –"Get the fuck out of here."*

Whenever she went through it in her mind, she had the final word.

What an odd name, "Belovski"! It could mean "Beloved" if one took away all hints at Eastern European roots. No trace of an accent, though. He could have been the one. But then the pathetic surprise! There had been no hint of paralysis in his voice. In fact, she'd thought of him as a tall, energetic man.

There was this one hidden thing, though. The piece of his manhood she'd possessed for a night. She'd warmed it up in her mouth, like some blubber rising in the ocean. Rising to the occasion. She'd sheltered it. Although he hadn't known it in his sleep, he'd trusted her. The jaw muscles were the most powerful of all. The safest was to keep laughing. Sometime during that night, she'd wished he could have walked out of there with her. *Where's your willpower!? Straighten up your limbs! Take control of your spine! Follow your prick to the end of the world.*

Hubert clearly wasn't the one. He wouldn't go anyplace soon. He would be stuck where he was for a while. Ilana slipped her nail file back into the bag. She closed the bag with a sigh. *If only that asshole Michael were less of a drag!*

CHAPTER 30

After the "escapade" with Ilana (which was the way Aunt Frieda referred to the night when his money had disappeared), Hubert's relationship with his aunt turned distinctly formal. There never had been much depth to their conversations, but rather some cordial understanding. Now, still with the memory of Ilana sitting in the kitchen at the maple table, Hubert could barely raise a smile on his aunt's face. He tried to humor her and asked questions about Toni and her goat, to no avail. Her answers were curt and to the point.

The most exciting change in his condition was marked by the arrival of the electric-powered wheelchair to replace his clumsy manual contraption. Since the village was laid out on hilly grounds (there was barely a road that was flat), he had been virtually trapped in the house. There was still no reply from Eric to his letter; Hubert felt deeply hurt by this. It was Aunt Frieda, again, despite the "escapade," who had found the solution. She had looked through several medical accessory catalogs until she'd found a special sale: the only model ever made with gears. It was cheap since the model was being discontinued.

"What do you want me to get?" he asked, propped up for the first time in the new Cadillac of wheelchairs. "I can do a real shopping trip now."

"Why don't you start small," Aunt Frieda said in a voice that had turned terse. "How about the bakery. We need some bread. And while you are at it, get some Sacher torte."

His first trip into the village started easy. The electric motor hummed, the gears shifted with delightful clicks, and he felt like traveling all the way to Vienna. But after crossing the street, aiming for the store, he discovered the curb was too high. He refused to consider the option of taking a trip alongside the curb in search for a ramp. For one, he would have been dangerously close to the traffic, and second, going back or along a loop would have felt like a defeat. But after a few tries, he had to ask two teenage boys who were passing along on the sidewalk to give him a hand. They were quite helpful but unsuccessful in estimating the center of gravity of wheelchair and occupant combined; the front wheel came up too high, and with surprising ease, the chair tipped backward, spilling Hubert onto the street. I'm nothing but a dead_chicken, he thought. He was able to ease the impact with his arms, which had developed powerful muscles from pushing the wheels of his old wheelchair, but he could not avoid getting his legs bruised. The two boys stared down at him with embarrassment and disbelief. The older one bent down:

"Is everything OK?" he asked.

"Not too bad," Hubert groaned. His legs, upper and lower parts, had fallen into impossible positions, like Mikado sticks, and just as in the game of Mikado, a major reshuffle was required for his limbs to be sorted out and put in order. The two helpers put the chair upright and lifted him into the seat. He thanked the boys profusely, but just after they left—not without uttering nervous apologies—he discovered they had put him back precisely where he had started before the fall. This time he followed the curb until he found a ramp.

As he looked once more into the window of the bakery, the unreachable goal, with its delicious *Prezn* and *Hupfn* and *Kuchen mit Schlag* on display, it struck him that since the age of five, he had never been so absolutely dependent on the goodwill of people around him. Certainly, in the eyes of the villagers, he was still someone who had "just arrived." On the time scale of the village, with its generations of solid farmers, petty poachers, and all the good people in between, a year counted as nothing. He sensed that ultimately, they would tolerate him just as they tolerated Tattering Fritz, who had cerebral palsy and lived with his sister Anna at the lower edge of the village, or Nudel-Joseph, a thirty-year-old with Down syndrome, who held his mother's hand and celebrated each successful crossing of the main street with giggles and a dance of joy. There were others in the village whose spirits had been crushed long ago in cruel family feuds and now lived their monosyllabic lives without demurring. Hubert feared that he might just be tolerated as an addition to this panopticon of abnormalities. The village needed a handsome collection of freaks as a warning for kids, telling them to be grateful because, after all, in this world, things can go terribly, morbidly wrong.

When he arrived back home, bruised and with dirty clothes, and his aunt asked him how he'd fared on this special day, he broke down. There was little he could do to stop his tears.

"Aunt Frieda, I have to talk to you," he said. "I've been thinking. I'm always taking. I never give anything back. Can I do something for you besides peeling apples? For the last, what, nine months?, I've been sitting in this wheelchair—well, it's been actually two, counting the time in both wheelchairs combined—thinking I deserve better. All along, I've been thinking: What an injustice to someone like me! And you know what? Maybe I really don't deserve better. I haven't earned any-thing. You've been like a mother to me, and I have done everything to make your life miserable. I'm sorry about this thing with Ilana. I mean, I loved every bit of it, but it was stupid."

"She is a whore," Aunt Frieda said with a flat, toneless voice. Her face had become tense at the mention of the escapade.

"OK, let's call her a whore. She said she's strictly a dancer, and dance is what she did, but for the purpose of our conversation, she can be a whore. I've been missing something. You know what I mean. I haven't been with a woman for ages. But the point is, what I really need most of all is someone to talk to, and I had it here all along. And missing out on it was stupid. I've been running away from something; I wish I knew what is wrong here inside."

"By bringing her here, you made my house filthy," his aunt said res-olutely. "I feel like hosing the walls down on the inside. I can't sit on my own couch anymore without thinking about the dirt you brought in."

"God, I'm sorry, OK?" Hubert said, exasperated. "What else do you want me to do now? I would help you scrub the floor and the walls if I could do it. And besides, I'm glad now she didn't touch the ceiling."

Aunt Frieda looked at him quietly and then stood and left the room. Hubert was shaking from the misunderstandings that were still piling up.

* * *

"Dear Eric:

you wanted me to travel, see the world. I felt it was almost a mission, as your alter ego. This letter is about failure. On a big scale. Things have not been easy. I'm sitting here, like a mirror of you on this side of the world, unable to walk. Today I fell on the street on my way to the bakery. It was pathetic. Two kids had to collect me and put me back into my wheelchair. And the letters I wrote to you before, about the hikes in the Alps? I never went on those trips. I just wanted you to think I was OK. But now you also know what the money was for. You never replied, and that's the part that hurts.

Your friend Hubert.

P.S. I hope soon, one of these days, we can have another beer at the Fountain."

* * *

That night, Hubert felt a sudden twinge in his left leg. Or was it only the physical memory of it? He was used to those phantom sensations, memories of feelings projected by his brain into old territory. But the new sensation was different, more intense. He tweaked his thigh—and felt a distant numb but needling touch. He lay motionless and held his breath. *Could it really be? The impact, the nerves… God knows, the body is so complicated, unpredictable. But if there were fifty-pound ovarian cysts in this world, then why not sudden rearrangements, regrowth in his spine?*

The doctor was called in; tests with needles were performed until the reemergence of sensation could be properly categorized. *There was a certain chance… there was this distinct possibility… although it was too early to speculate…* The tiresome lingo of the profession, which attaches words to the different shadows of doubt! Just as on the long day on the train, when it all happened, Hubert felt as though he were surrounded by haze, as if transgressing an invisible wall but now going in the opposite direction.

He was afraid of hoping for chances, distinct possibilities. After the doctor's visit, Hubert decided to guard the stirring of new life in his legs as a secret. He feared they might be destroyed by broadcasting, just as love is known to be in its first tender stage. He went in seclusion and spent most of his time behind the curtain, watching through the filigree of the fabric the unsteady migration of clouds over the Hundertzack. Although he watched this movement intently, he knew he was unable to shift his inner eye away from one particular muscle in his right thigh. It is strange, he thought, the way things happen! What he didn't realize before the accident on the curb he now saw with great clarity: that he'd been almost ready to live in the narrowing circles of Austria's hinterland, the village, and his wheelchair, that he'd been ready to accept the idea of a life spent in the bliss of innocence. It was the kind of life he had always looked down on with contempt: the life of one of those brown cows in the pasture.

* * *

"I don't want to see him."

"It's Herr Krantz, though. I told him."

"Told him what? This nonsense with my legs?"

Peter entered with bouncing steps, a white carnation in his lapel, one arm hidden behind his back.

"Con-grat-u-la-tions!" he exclaimed theatrically as if addressing an entire audience. "What wonderful news!"

"Peter? Didn't Frieda tell you? I need some rest."

"Rest, of course, rest assured: rest will be provided. But let us first celebrate." With this, he stepped forth, smiled broadly, and produced a bottle of Champagne with the hand that had been hidden.

Hubert groaned like a wounded animal.

"Don't you understand?" he said. "Why are you doing this to me? How can I celebrate a twitch, a stir? It's like confusing a firefly with the light at the end of a tunnel. I can't blame you, dear Aunt Frieda. You are a bundle of hope; you're made like that. You cling to straws; you pull yourself from one day to the other. But Peter, you are a schoolteacher. You are a learned man. You should know better. Champagne? Didn't it occur to you that... if things go wrong, there'll be a bitter aftertaste forever?

Aunt Frieda's eyes filled with tears. She hid her face in her hands and sobbed.

"Hubert, how can you say things like that? Herr Krantz and Toni and everyone in this village mean so well. They respect you. They see you struggle. They're struggling *with* you, do you understand?"

Peter stood next to her awkwardly.

"Sorry. I really thought you'd appreciate it. I better go." He walked toward the door, and then, hesitating, he placed the bottle on the table without making any sound before he turned, ready to leave the room.

"Peter, wait!" Hubert said as he saw another turbulence unfold. "I'm sorry. I'm having a hard time. I'm frightened, I guess. I shouldn't be ashamed of it. There is so much that can go wrong. Please stay! I appreciate your coming. Let's do something with this bottle."

"OK, I'll get some glasses," Peter said.

"The cherry cupboard in the kitchen," Aunt Frieda said to Peter. "Two shelves up on the left-hand side. Take the good ones."

"What an honor," Hubert exclaimed. "The good crystal glasses!"

Aunt Frieda said, "You know, when you arrived back in October last year, you were in bad shape. The villagers watched you being carried in. They followed the comings and goings of doctors anxiously. They are basically good people. They take an interest in you, they suffered with you, and you must give something back to them. Don't close yourself up now; let them share your little triumphs, too."

Hubert listened to her with his hands covering his face. He sighed.

Peter returned with the crystal glasses and popped the Champagne bottle. He proposed a toast:

"To the central nervous system of my cosmopolitan friend!"

"Prost," said Aunt Frieda, raising her glass to the other two.

"Prosit," Hubert said. "Honestly. I don't know where I would be without you folks."

CHAPTER 31

In the package was one of the fruits of Eric's business; Hubert could feel it through the soft red paper it was wrapped in. When he had peeled the paper off, he held in his hand an almost weightless leprous-looking head: black spots marring a dark-green sculpture of a head with high cheekbones and wide-set eyes. Its skin was shriveled and rough. The thing looked as though an overgrown, overripe avocado had come to life. He felt his heartbeat as he stared at the morbid apparition: he realized that he was looking at a disintegrating version of his own face. There was an envelope at the bottom of the package, containing a letter, a single page. From the date, it was clear Eric had not received the last letter Hubert had sent. Hubert opened it with unsteady hands and read:

Dear Hubert:

So good to hear from you! I hate to break the news. I know you need the money back. But things have not been well. Did you read about the hail? There's never been hail like that in this part of the country. Golf-ball sized; it was on the national news. Well, as you can imagine, the greenhouse is badly damaged, and most of the crop is gone. We tried to rescue what we could (Stewart has been terrific!), but only one out of five had even made contact with the molds; the rest were just plain small gourds, worth nothing. Hubert, I don't have the money now to give back to you. I still owe Stewart two paychecks. Things will look up as soon as we have the glass repaired and the new seedlings in.

(My sister has been a pest. The man she dated is gone, and Jane takes it out on me. I also owe her a lot of money now.)

I wish I could get out of here someday and travel all over like you, but I guess now this has to wait for a while.

All the best,
Eric.

P.S. There's a lot of partying going on in your house. I wonder if any-body's told you. These guys put a couch on the front porch, beige and brown striped. I wonder if it's yours? It gets wet there, not to mention the bugs.

Hubert felt the urge to laugh even though he just learned that his ten grand was gone. There were no beige-and-brown-striped couch in his possession. Whatever this monstrous piece of furniture was, it could rot on his porch; it was not his concern. The parties were a more serious matter. He decided to send a note to Rich, his technician, asking him to do some checking. But the world of Eric's green experiments was now so remote. *"Golf balls!"* he murmured. *"Travel like you! New seedlings in! Old seedlings out!"*

* * *

It was early summer—the snow on the Hundertzack had receded, leaving only caps. The scent of herbs was strong in the air. Back in the States, on the East Coast, spring was the time of definition: the growth of the plants was precise and directed, and the shoots had the light-green color of innocence. Summer was the time when all the available space was filled and colors reached saturation; all that could be decently done in this climate had been duly accomplished. (August, of course, was the time of exuberance. The plants went beyond their mission, entangling one another as if drunk; they became careless and invited invasions of caterpillars and bugs, the first signs of decay.) Here in the Alps, the vegetation was more careful, less daring. It was as if spring was in reality spread over three seasons, to be killed by the early snow, well before summer could make a glorious appearance.

Hubert had nurtured the stirrings of his nerves under the strict protocol of his specialist; he'd been in water therapy every day and had regained some control over his legs. It couldn't yet exactly be called walking, but the prognosis was good. In his bed, he was able to curl up and dream about moving like a seagull in the sky.

* * *

One day, toward the end of June, he received a postcard from Spain. Victor and his wife were vacationing at the Costa del Sol. "Topless makes me speechless," his sparse handwriting said. Hubert could see Victor adding these lines on his way to the mailbox, safely out of reach of his wife. He sighed and turned the postcard over. The usual fishing harbor scene: a romantic niche cut out (by a clever choice of viewing point and angle) from a town that, to his knowledge, had cement-mixing machines running on every roadblock and that was about to be drowned in concrete.

Oh, yes, Victor!—the night in the unruly seaside bars had transformed him from a distant memory into a fat, perspiring, jovial drinking companion. But then he had just as quickly disappeared from Hubert's vision. How was it that after a lapse of a few years, friends could never again be what they used to be? Reflecting on that night after his fateful trip to Austria, he had decided that the Victor of Klabaasters and Beesters had been no more real than a ghost.

A small boat on the postcard caught his attention; it looked oddly familiar, although he'd never been to Spain. And then he suddenly realized that the boat in front of Hotel Aan Zee had presented a similar angle when the bird had tried to lure him away. It had been the moment when he'd resisted a magic call, when he had poo-poohed the attempt of a creature-messenger to nudge him into a new direction. He had been deaf, like so many times before. "Don't blame me," a thunderous voice might yet tell him someday. "I gave you a chance." And he, Hubert, would have nothing to say but mumble apologies about a profound misunderstanding of signs, about the necessity of a sender to prepare a receiver for truly new information, about the way his job had been bungled, and Moses's hadn't, and crazy things like that.

The postcard seemed to say, without spelling it out, "It's not too late." But how would Victor know? He popped the postcard up on his nightstand. When he switched the little table lamp on, the boat was flooded with a wide streak of light and looked as if it were immersed in the early-morning sun and ready to reveal its secrets. *It's not too late*, he said to himself over and over again, and he vowed to return to the very place of bifurcation as soon as his condition allowed it.

CHAPTER 32

The air was hazy, and the buildings lining the empty Sunday morning streets of Scheveningen were colored in pastel tones.

"They can't do this," Hubert exclaimed as the taxi came to a halt. The Aan Zee hotel had entirely disappeared, and in its place was a ghastly building with an art nouveau façade, housing a cinema called Spleen. Pink and jade green tiles were set in flowery ornaments, which appeared to spill into the sky. A billboard in front of it depicted a man, with a gun in his hand and a grin on his face, who was embracing a woman with his free arm. The smoke emerging from the gun, hinting at its most recent use, was delicately curled, as though in celebration of some success. What Hubert had liked and respected about Helga was her fierce independence. Their courtship had been mutual both times. The billboard seemed to convey the opposite message: conquer by force, laugh in your triumph, and keep the pressure up.

Aan Zee, in its peaceful coexistence with the town around it and with the world, was now a mere memory. What had once bothered him as inconvenient imperfections—the labyrinth design, the total absence of ergonomic considerations, the capricious style of management, the imposition of ever-changing rules—struck him now as qualities quintessentially human. The loss of the hotel, the place where he'd last seen his parents, was an unacceptable, incomprehensible quirk of fate. In the absence of any other material correlate, Aan Zee had also stood for the culmination of his love. Its erasure and replacement by a theatre was nothing less than a callous, heinous act against humanity.

"They can't? Sure they can," the taxi driver said. "They did all sorts of things. They even closed the Northern Sun."

"They what? They closed it? The nudist club?"

"Yes. That one."

"What happened? Let me guess: a scandal involving an act of obscenity."

"Close," the driver chuckled. "Somebody, a member of the public looking through the fence, spotted an erection." He was a heavyset man with a bulky red nose, and he seemed to take great pleasure in relating this story.

"Oh no!" Hubert chuckled. "A real-life erection! How inconsiderate! How obscene!"

He paid for his fare but asked the driver to wait. With hesitating steps—each one was still an effort—he crossed the promenade and descended the stairway to the beach. Walking in the sand proved difficult. He was no longer able to negotiate the quick slippage of the sand under his feet. His cane poked into the ground without finding much purchase. Aware of the sad spectacle his balancing act would present to an onlooker, he slowly made his way to the place where he'd once seen the boat. He used the big sign of the movie theater as a landmark to gauge his position, remembering that he'd followed the bird to the left for some distance. Hubert was sure he couldn't be off by more than twenty yards, yet from the point he was standing at, he could not see anything resembling a boat.

Following a sudden impulse, he turned and walked back toward the taxi. Before he reached the stairway, he could see through the open window of the car that the driver had reclined his seat; ready to take a nap.

"Listen, I changed my mind!" Hubert shouted. "This will take some time. You just move on." The driver stretched, readjusted his seat, and acknowledged the new order with a sign of his hand.

Hubert returned to the approximate spot of former magic, sat down, and closed his eyes. *"Rip van Winkel,"* he mumbled to himself. *"A rip-off of the past. Requiescat in pace. May the past rest in peace."*

Someone behind him cleared his throat—a woman, he guessed, from the pitch of the sound.

He heard a raspy, almost crowing voice: "Are you all right?"

"Of course I am. What is this about?" Hubert responded, surprised and irritated as he turned around and saw a short official-looking man in his fifties with a head like a pumpkin. Something was funny about his nose. It was pointed in a strange way.

"We have loitering laws in Scheveningen," the man said in his high-pitched voice. "This is something new, you know. But too many things have happened here on the beach. Drugs, for instance. I'm sure you understand. People are in church on Sunday at this hour."

He was clad in some type of uniform bearing the emblem of the city, but it was crumpled and sprinkled with a red substance that looked very much like pasta sauce.

This here is *my* church, Hubert was tempted to reply. "All right," he said instead. "You want to know why I'm here? Because I've got the use of my legs again. My legs are back in business. You understand?"

The Scheveningen security guard stared back at him for a second and then nodded politely.

"You seem fine. I'm sure you're clean. Just checking." He continued his lonely patrol, whistling. After a few steps, he turned around and asked, "did you lose something?"

"Come to think of it, I guess I did," Hubert replied, laughing sarcastically. He bent down—it was quite a balancing act—picked up a handful of sand, and threw it into the air, feeling like a little boy who is tired of building castles. Then he walked slowly back toward the road. When the man had shrunk to the size of a small matchstick in the distance, Hubert again remembered another moment from long ago, when a small, feathered creature had disappeared into the morning mist.

CHAPTER 33

Hubert found himself in a stately room with enormously high ceilings. Through the open windows came the sounds of bells from a nearby church and a sweet smell. He was sitting in a leather armchair, opposite an old man dressed in a black suit. The old man directed his speech at him. He wore a wig and a white beard, and what could be seen of the skin of his face was white as chalk. His half-opened eyes and his slouched position on the Turkish sofa gave him a slightly condescending look; it made him appear as if he considered the business that had brought Hubert into his office a mere trifling matter. When he started to speak in a snarling voice, this impression was at once contradicted by a tone of urgency. Something else was odd: his lips did not move—he barely opened his mouth.

"You are not alone, my young friend," he said. "You are not alone with your dreams. We all have thought of this eternal breakfast: the big table, the windows half-open, the curtains moving in the soft breeze of early summer, a honeydew smell in the air; our friends—past, present, and future—seated on two sides of the long table in perfect serendipity, sipping coffee and engaged in animated conversation. A scantily dressed girl arrives—the black lace of her vaudeville costume both confining and revealing swelling parts of her young body. She is today's singing telegram, and if you listen carefully (and why would you not?) and give her a five-dollar bill at the right moment, toward the end of her act, you will hear your own fortune sung. She tucks the five-dollar bill underneath the seam of her costume and begins her chant."

Hubert listened to the monologue as though in a trance. He could firmly see himself in the scene the old man described; his mind added a yellow butterfly that drifted by outside the open window in a tumbling motion. What appeared in the distance beyond were the green, rolling, breathing hills of the Helderbergs. He knew his precise place at the table—in the middle seat on the right—and from here, he staked the geometry of his glances: Helga and Karen sitting at the opposite side of the table, separated from each other by two male guests—two class-mates from high school with inconsequential smiles on their still-pim-pled faces. Thus, his old-time girlfriends formed two vibrating apexes at the base of a triangle that included him as the third. In this newly found space he let his eyes wander; from the pictures on the walls to the waiters and waitresses standing at attention, until they arrived with a shock on the costume of the singing telegram: this was a man, as sure as he, Hubert, was one himself. His eyes wandering upward, he recognized Eric, who bared his teeth in a big grin.

"Hearing your fortune told," the sage continued, now with his eyes almost closed, "you smile, and it proves contagious. It travels up and down the table and jumps across, and soon the entire room is filled with the single beam of your smile."

At these last words, a transformation took place: the old man's beard shrank by half an inch, and the high ceiling of the room receded even further, as though these two measures were linked by a formula of divine proportion. Clouds drifted across the ceiling as though part of an elaborate stage design; but then, looking up and straining his eyes, Hubert could no longer make out a physical boundary separating the room from the outside space.

"What are you waiting for?" the old man said. "This is all I have to say. You seem surprised. What, after all, is the gender of the mind? A good evening to you, sir. Good luck. Dismissed."

Hubert rose from his chair and thanked the man profusely. "But before you leave, tell me, what is your name?" he asked.

"Kannitverstahn," was the answer.

Notes by the Author

This novel started with an exercise in writing fiction almost forty years ago, in William Kennedy's fiction writing class at the Albany Public Library. I remember turning in a short story, entitled "Aan Zee," which was the seed of what has become Chapter 4 in this novel—the convoluted journey inside the hotel from the reception area to the protagonist's assigned room. Kennedy gave me praise for it and urged me to expand the short story into a novel.

Yes, the story started with a real conference I was invited to in The Hague, and yes, the setting of the first chapter is inspired by the monolithic architecture of the Empire State Plaza in Albany, but everything else is pure fiction, even the topic of the conference and even Aunt Frieda, the puritan well-meaning aunt in the Austrian Alps.

—Joachim Frank, August 30, 2019, New York.

Two previous editions of this novel were published under bizarre circumstances, involving—as I recently found out with the help of a lawyer—a contract with a person claiming to represent a press that had ceased to exist long before as a legal entity. This first legitimate edition is a revised version of the original manuscript.

—Joachim Frank, July 23, 2025, New York

About the Author

Joachim Frank is a German-born scientist and a writer living in New York. He has published numerous poems, prose poems and short stories (see franxfiction.com) and one novel, *Ierapetra, or His Sister's Keeper*. He is a Professor at Columbia University. In 2017 he shared the Nobel Prize in Chemistry with Jacques Dubochet and Richard Henderson.

www.ingramcontent.com/pod-product-compliance
Lightning Source LLC
Chambersburg PA
CBHW021959130726
47903CB00014B/2488